Praise for Roisín O

'Roisín O'Donnell is among the most talented of the new generation that are extending the range of the Irish short story and updating it for a twenty-first-century readership. Reading her is like picking through a treasure trove of the human imagination – you can't but be enriched by it. Highly recommended.'

– Dave Lordan

'Roisin O'Donnell breaks the bounds of the short story… O'Donnell has innovated with a texture and depth not often encountered in the short form.'

– Deidre Conroy, *Sunday Independent*

'This impeccably written story is magnificently structured; the language is witty and intelligent, and every so often you find yourself shaking your head in amazement at how O'Donnell captures a fleeting feeling.'

– Berni Dwan

'O'Donnell shapes a bittersweet sad comedy that is an absolute masterpiece.'

– *San Diego Book Review*

'Roisín O'Donnell is playful and exuberant in her approach to the multi-racial society Ireland is becoming.'

– *The Times Literary Supplement*

'O'Donnell's assured writing mixes shifts in pace and tense seamlessly.'

— *Minor Literatures*

'The poetry is lush and poignant in the prose of Bennett and Roisín O'Donnell.'

— Anne O'Neil, *Headstuff*

'[O'Donnell] delicately intuits a metaphor, which resonates throughout the collection, for the complexities of a nation increasingly not at home with itself.'

— *The Times Literary Supplement*

'I first ran across her work in the *Young Irelanders* anthology released earlier this year. At the time I thought, "Holy Jaysus, there's another Dorothy Parker been born." Infinite Landscapes reinforces that judgement.'

— Hubert O'Hearn

'I love the style of this story: a series of things learnt, some obvious, some less so; a gradual supplanting of hope with hard certainties. It's intelligent, involving and beautifully written.'

— Donal Ryan

'From the rich, luxurious language of love to the bleak austerity of Loch con Nualla ... an amazingly skilled and talented author with a freshness and vitality in every sentence.'

— Garry Bannister

WILD QUIET

Roisín O'Donnell

NEW ISLAND

WILD QUIET
First published in 2016
by
New Island Books,
16 Priory Hall Office Park,
Stillorgan,
County Dublin.
Republic of Ireland.

www.newisland.ie

PRINT ISBN: 978-1-84840-500-4
EPUB ISBN: 978-1-84840-501-1
MOBI ISBN: 978-1-84840-502-8

British Library Cataloguing Data.
A CIP catalogue record for this book is available from the British Library.

Typeset by JVR Creative India
Cover design by Karen Vaughan
Printed by ScandBook AB

New Island received financial assistance from The Arts Council (*An
Chomhairle Ealaíon*), 70 Merrion Square, Dublin 2, Ireland.

10 9 8 7 6 5 4 3 2 1

For Mam and Dad,
for everything

Contents

Ebenezer's Memories

I first found out about him during one of the Christmases we spent in Derry in the mid 1990s, when I was six or seven and my brother, Jack, was four or five. We'd been playing hide-and-seek in Grandad's red-brick terrace, when Jack had hidden in the cupboard under the stairs and I'd got lost between numbers on my countdown from a hundred, and had forgotten (probably deliberately) to find my brother until it was nearly teatime. By then, woolly dust was clinging to Jack's flaxen hair. His eyes were so red from crying that his irises blazed technicolour blue. His face was so dirty that he resembled a *Mary Poppins* chimney sweep.

Mammy sat us down on Grandad's hard brown sofa and shouted, 'Catherine. Jack. Yous are never, never, never to play in that cupboard again! What would your dad say? God rest him. Of all the places in this bloody house ...'.

'Maggie,' Grandad put a hand on Mammy's shoulder, 'go an' stick the kettle on. Let me have a word with these two.'

Wiping her eyes on the cuff of her sleeve, Mammy turned in to the kitchen.

Grandad sighed, as if heavily burdened by the weight of the forthcoming conversation, and eased himself down onto the rocking chair. Damp black socks laddered the white radiator behind him, making it look like a melting piano. From the scullery came the hiss of the kettle and the mustiness of boiling spuds. Grandad smoothed his corduroys with hands leathery from a life spent delivering oil around the farms of Ulster, from Lisnaskea to Cushendall, from Castlewellan to Dungiven. He adjusted his heavy glasses, leaned forward and whispered, 'Now then. Can yous two keep a secret?'

Our heads bopped like the novelty nodding pup in the back window of our family Fiesta, and Grandad checked over his shoulders both ways, twice. This was the way of my storytelling grandfather. A veteran with a never-spoken-of limp dating back to the battle of El Alamein, who would stand outside Aunt Ruby's kitchen window, double check to make sure I was watching, and carefully eat one of her prize lemon roses, petal by petal. Who, years later, when I was informed at school about *the Birds and the Bees*, promptly led me up the yard and pointed out with great authority the gorse bush under which he'd found me when I'd been delivered by Norwegian stork one starless September night.

'Let me tell yous,' Grandad whispered, 'there's a monster living in that cupboard—stop pickin' your nose, Jack—and his name is Ebenezer.'

Jack wiped his nose on the back of his skinny wrist, 'Aww, Grandad.'

'You think I'm jokin', Jack Donnelly?' Grandad shook his head. 'Did ye not hear somethin' scary when you were in there? Think about it now, Jack. Think really carefully.'

My brother chewed his lower lip. Cupboard dust and grime streaked his forehead, turning his narrow face into a charcoal sketch. Being a bit of a daydreamer, my credulity was instant, but Jack was already less willing to believe. Behind the distorting blur of his heavy lenses, Grandad's small eyes flashed the unexpected blue of a kingfisher on a riverbank. His sincerity was palpable; you could practically inhale it.

'Maybe…' Jack conceded, 'yeah, maybe I did.'

'So ye heard it?' Grandad gave a single nod. 'Aye. That's coz Ebenezer's hungry. I've to feed him newspapers every day, and other things. What things, Catherine? Scary things, pet. Things we'd rather forget. But do yous know what his favourite thing to eat is?'

We shook our heads, and Grandad leaned closer. 'His favourite snack is wee wains from England. So yous are not to go playin' in that cupboard again, understand?'

The arthritic brass pendulum of the fireplace clock wheezed the half hour. As if the chimes had broken the spell of his storytelling, Grandad stood. 'Now then.' Readjusting his glasses, he pottered into the kitchen, whistling the opening refrain of 'Be Thou My Vision', leaving Jack and me in a silence so thick we could have swum right through it.

The next day, a bitter December afternoon, I was hopscotching down Glendermot Road when I overheard Miss Annie from number 46 say to Miss Carmichael from number 3, 'There's that poor wain from the *Mixed Marriage*.'

'And the daddy. Mercy on his soul.'

I stumbled over a pavement crack, suddenly feverish in my duffle coat. I wanted to cry, but instead I gritted my molars and shoved my fists into my pockets. A feeling like fear made my pulse quicken, and the moment was stored in my memory as a hurt foretold, something that upset me now and would anger me later, in a way I didn't yet understand.

Mixed Marriage. I continued skipping, reminded of cake mix and the way my Granny Nora's ruddy elbows used to work the batter like pistons.

Things we'd rather forget. I fastened the toggles of my coat up to my chin and hurried back to number twelve, trailing my skipping rope behind me.

I'd never found it odd that none of my aunts, uncles or cousins appeared in my parents' wedding album. I'd always presumed that all weddings featured a London street, bell-bottom trousers, a skinny tie, an ivory dress with three-quarter-length sleeves, and a total of four wedding guests. After my parents eloped to England, both families refused to speak to them. Letters went unanswered. Phone calls rang into silence. The families remained locked in a stand-off that lasted nearly a decade.

Jack and I were still toddlers when Dad died, at which point my grandparents finally got back in touch. Soon after, Mammy moved the family to Sheffield, returning to Derry each Christmas and almost every summer to visit my two surviving grandparents. We'd visit Granny Donnelly, who was ensconced in the mahogany darkness of St Augustine's Nursing Home, on a wind-scoured hill in Rosemount. But we'd always stay with Grandad Williamson, who lived in the treeless maze of the Waterside. With steely resolve, Mammy maintained our tradition of visiting Derry, no matter what. Once or twice a year she'd wake us in the 'wee small hours' and we'd journey overnight, through the larynx of England and the tonsils of Scotland, arriving in the bleak Stranraer dawn for the early crossing to Larne.

Derry was a city visited rarely enough for it to have retained its mythical quality in my imagination. In the absence of schoolbook histories, my sense of Derry's past was woven from family legends. I'd heard about the scuttled U-boats in the Foyle basin, and I imagined them trawling the dark. The city walls, intact and off-limits, knotted a noose around the town centre. Under dripping archways, dank with moss and lichen, my footsteps bounced back at me. The 'City of Oaks', on whose dark corners angels whispered, could change her mood as quickly as light shifted on the Foyle.

Compared to the open horizons of the seven-hilled English city where we were being raised, Derry was a secretive place, full of fenced-off quarters. Corrugated sheets of khaki metal shielded Ebrington Barracks. Concrete warehouses fortified the deserted docklands, where Dad had gone for an early run on the last morning of his life. A canopy of dark-leafed sycamores cloaked the north bank of the river. Even when viewed in panorama from St Columb's Park, the city seemed to shrink from view, hidden by an illusion of the soft grey light, the angle of the low-lying hills.

A few days later, an overcast morning in the unwrapped wake of Christmas, Jack and I had been playing hospital, but my useless brother had fallen asleep on the sofa, leaving me alone with a pram of half-bandaged teddies. Mammy had gone into the town to pick up something in the January sales, and Grandad was milling about the yard, humming 'How Great Thou Art' whilst clipping back the ivy on the backyard wall.

Alone, I squiggled my name in the condensation on the living-room window and watched the letters stream into each other. With a technique developed through many years of painful practice, I carefully climbed onto the back of the rocking chair, balancing to manage its sway, and sneaked a Mikado biscuit from the Bovril tin above the wireless. Next, I had a go at winding and unwinding the mangle in the scullery, which Grandad said was used for squeezing the badness out of bold wains. Entertainment options exhausted, I climbed upstairs and sat on the hard single bed, where Mammy and Aunt Ruby had slept as wains, their nocturnal battles making Grandad threaten to put a plank down the centre of the bed to separate them.

It was as I sat swinging my legs, chewing the end of my braid and imagining a bed with a pine plank down the centre that I first heard it: a low moan, with the sadness of whale song, drawn out and muffled as if reaching me from across oceans, yet close enough to make the windowpanes shiver. It got louder and louder, like a train tunnelling under the house. And again that low moan sounded; the saddest, lowest echo you can imagine.

Clinging to the bannister, trying to avoid the steps that creaked, I climbed back down the stairs. In the hall the sound was like the warning groan of a foghorn from a floundering ship. With my heart in my throat, I traced the sound to the cupboard under the stairs. As I knelt, the groans stopped and were replaced by a crashing growl, like waves pounding the rocks of Magilligan Strand. And there was a pulse inside the sound, a watery, pre-natal heartbeat, the paced and laboured breathing of something waiting to flee or to pounce.

My hand reached for the cupboard door of its own accord while I watched with the helplessness of nightmares. The door was locked, but my fingers slipped under the crack at its bottom. I winced, expecting something sharp, the quick gnash of teeth. Instead, a cold head rush spread over me, the chill experienced when you've been caught lying. A tug, like when you stand in the surf at high tide and feel the sand dragged from under you. I felt a sudden dizziness, and dots of blue danced before my eyes, like the wake of a camera flash. Blue turned to blazing white and then cleared into flickering light-filled images.

It was as if the moving pictures were being projected inside my eyelids from an invisible cinema reel. I saw half-remembered faces, and others I had only seen in photographs. Looking closely into the fan of light, I saw Grandad manning the big guns. I felt the breath, tight in his chest, the sweat stinging his eyes. I felt his lurch of terror as three Luftwaffe planes appeared on the horizon, the flares of their ammunition trained on the spot where Grandad's five Waterside pals were manning another set of artillery. I saw the black sheen of the big guns, and felt the still desert night stretching in all directions. Through Grandad's eyes, I felt momentum dragging me towards the magnet of a terrible moment. But the desert images then became spotted with purple light, so all I could see were the whites of eyeballs and pieces of somebody's knees.

Blinking, I saw other images so small it was hard to work out what they were. There was a shard of black metal, which turned out to be the helm of a surrendered U-boat, towed into the Foyle with drowned German sailors inside. In another flickering film of images, an iridescent orb turned out to be a button on my dad's polo shirt as he knelt to tie his laces before his morning run. I saw him pausing on his way out of the cheap hotel room to check on the cots where Jack and I lay sleeping. I realised that I must have been seeing our parents' first time back in Derry since they had eloped. I felt the pride swelling in my dad's chest. And as I watched, his shirt button turned into the moon, floating above the Arcadia Dance Hall on the night my parents met.

Again the images shifted, and I heard my Granny Nora's laughter and smelt her fresh-baked soda bread. I saw my mammy getting ready for a date, twisting her hair into a bun on the top of her head and turning to my Aunt Ruby. 'How do I look?' On and on the images came. When the vertigo-inducing montage made me dizzy, I pulled back my hand, from which the blood had drained almost entirely.

Spots of blue and purple light faded into white, and the hall became visible. Sounds from within the cupboard subsided, and all I could hear was the ticking of the grandfather clock and the lull of traffic from the road outside. As my pulse steadied, there was a stilling in me, a levelling off of emotions as fear morphed into relief. It was like that moment when you wake from a nightmare and it takes a few minutes to readjust to reality. My ears rang, and I kept recalling Grandad's words: 'Things we'd rather forget.' And I gradually began to realise that as well as being a great devourer of unwanted newspapers, Ebenezer was a fairly ferocious consumer of unwanted memories too.

Hardly believing what I had seen, I stumbled to the sofa where Jack lay sleeping with his mouth wide open. I cuddled up next to my brother and plunged into the type of murky sleep from which the sleeper emerges exhausted.

A long while later I awoke, hungry, remembering nothing of my dreams.

It was always on lonely afternoons that the sound would come, calling me back to Ebenezer's cupboard once again. No one else could hear Ebenezer's calls, which thrilled and terrified me. Each time I slipped my fingers under the door, blue dots would dance and turn to white, and I'd witness episodes of family history, like snatches of a stolen documentary.

The images and sounds I witnessed were gnarled and broken things, almost impossible to decipher. A sudden rush of blood on the petunias could have been the first baby

Aunt Ruby lost. But it could just as easily have been Granny Donnelly's tears staining the roses on my dad's coffin. Because each scene was crackly and fizzled towards its close, I decided that Ebenezer had been chewing these images, that what I witnessed were his leftovers, so gloopy and well-chewed they often melted into each other. Mammy's orange miniskirt and auburn beehive ('How do I look?') had become knotted up with army razor wire. Two cats fighting in the yard had become bullets ricocheting through the quiet of the docklands.

No one believed in Ebenezer, only me and Grandad. He lived in the cupboard under the stairs and waited for Grandad to breathe in the door and feed him his memories. Waiting, Ebenezer cowered like a cud-chewing Friesian in the dark, gnawing love letters down to their syllables. He didn't know how he'd got there, or who he was before he existed. I was his chance of escape, and each winter he felt me coming from across the water to ask Grandad strange questions. How come Granny Donnelly doesn't like Mammy? How come we have to live in England? Why can't we stay in Derry with you?

To Ebenezer, my voice was soothing. Grandad's replies trembled like autumn branches hassled by the wind. And when I slipped my fingers under the cupboard door, Ebenezer jangled the broken charms of his memory scraps. He knew that I would set him free. He knew this because I was more nosy than afraid.

Each winter morning I would watch Grandad scraping the fireplace clean, fetching coal from Ebenezer's cupboard— 'Stay there now, Catherine, careful Ebenezer doesn't catch sight of ye'—and feeding Ebenezer the previous week's *Londonderry Sentinel* or *Derry Journal*.

But in all these mornings of watching and waiting, and all the furtive minutes spent with my cheek to the rough red carpet, peering under the cupboard door, I never saw Ebenezer himself. I imagined him scaled like a dragon, dredged up from the Foyle, with the river's misty mornings still reflecting in his eyes. I knew he had sharp teeth; with these he had made mincemeat of my family's unwanted memories. And I knew he had a heartbeat.

When we returned to Derry, it was summer. And until that summer of '98, I thought Northern Ireland was just something that happened on the TV. It was something that would surface between the construction of the Millennium Dome, the investigation into the death of Princess Diana, and ads for Cornflakes and baked beans. The Troubles were confined to the six o'clock news, after which the weather woman would stand with the left shoulder of her suit blocking out the republic. Northern Ireland had nothing to do with Grandad's house, which we continued to visit each Christmas and almost every summer.

And yet in that summer of '98 I began to notice things about Derry that I hadn't heeded before. The grey rainbow of the New Bridge arced across the Foyle. Bands of red-white-and-blue paint wrapped the kerbs of the Waterside to the point of strangulation. Stripes of green-white-and-orange lined the pavements of Rosemount. The skull of a paramilitary was painted on a gable-end near Grandad's house with the words *No surrender* written on a scroll above it. A tricolour tied to a machine gun adorned a gable-end at Rosemount, and the words *You are now entering Free Derry* guarded the Bogside. Checkpoints were manned by British soldiers cradling long black rifles, their eyes scanning the area just above our heads.

I'd grown taller by that summer, all elbows and knees, flowery leggings and a jumper with a pink mouse on it. As soon as we arrived at Grandad's house, I knelt by Ebenezer's cupboard and placed my ear against the door. 'Catherine, what are you at?' Mammy asked.

I jumped back, 'Just messin'.'

And Grandad watched on, knowing, but saying nothing. He knew Ebenezer's breath could corrode the memory of a face down to its outline. Ebenezer was always hungry because Grandad never fed him enough memories, and always flatulent because those memories were tough to digest. Poor Ebenezer, it must have been terrible always to be this gassy. One belch and a kneecap shattered. One fart and a petrol bomb exploded across the Foyle. He wanted to leave Grandad's cupboard and breathe his memories back to their owners, but he was trapped, hungering for that which poisoned him.

Lying by Grandad's hearth one August morning, reading the *Beano* while Mammy sliced stacks of sandwiches to bring to the beach, I was jolted out of my daydream by an outburst from Ebenezer's cupboard—a sound so different from his previous noises that it sent goosebumps crawling up my arms, like an army of ice-legged ants creeping over my skin. I looked around for Grandad to see if he was hearing this too. But I then remembered that he was upstairs napping; older now, and less prone to fits of storytelling.

This time there were no growls and whines. Instead, a type of vocalised heartbreak seemed to originate, not just from the foundations of Grandad's house, but from the belly of the hills on which the city of Derry stood.

Tiptoeing into the hall, I knelt by the cupboard and listened. Tortured groans came from within: the whimpering of an animal with a fractured bone or a limb torn from it.

What had Ebenezer eaten? The unsayable and unsaid. Which memory had finally made him sick to his stomach so he couldn't eat any more?

I tugged at the brass latch of the cupboard door, and to my fright it gave way a little. It rocked on its rusty nails, creaking in slight complaint as the brass hinge bent. For the first time the blistering door opened a chink, through which I could peek.

Again came the dots of purple, blue, and then a blazing white glare. The memories were fuller now, and I was standing in the middle of them. The faces were sharper and less mottled, as if Ebenezer had found them impossible to chew.

I saw my dad running in bluish docklands light, proud to be home in Derry for the first time in a decade, and wondering what Granny Donnelly would say if he were just to turn up on her doorstep with the two wains. What would she say? Surely she'd be pleased. Maggie had begged him not to run until it got light. 'Derry's changed, Gerard,' she'd said. 'We don't know the city now, so we don't.' But he hadn't run for a fortnight and was getting out of shape. He'd never make the Sheffield Marathon at this rate, and there'd be no chance to run later once the kids were up and about.

The image faded, and I saw my dad's brown eyes losing focus. His body slumping, not in a crisp-sheeted hospital bed as Mammy had described it to me, but in a docklands alley. I felt the life ebb out of him, his blood wet and dark as ink. He stared right at me, as if seeing through my skull. I wanted to pull my hand back, to step out of the memory, but I couldn't.

Heart threatening to burst like a smashed piñata, I blinked and saw Mammy kneeling by the electric fire and telling Grandad, 'Dad, I've met someone.' I felt their joint fear, the heat of the fire on their faces. Grandad knowing before she continues, in the way some stories are known before they are heard, that the boy is Catholic. His silent tears were made horrific by the reddish hue of the electric fire. I saw bars of brightness ticking as they cooled, and felt Mammy aching with love for him. For my dad. For both of them.

Blinking again, I saw the Trinity knot tattooed on my dad's shoulder. Nothing more. Just his shoulder. This close-up lasted and lasted, until the sense of doom that welled up in me was unbearable.

At that moment, the brass handle in my hand became light. As the cupboard door broke from its hinge, an unholy roar sent me scarpering backwards on all fours, crab-like on the maroon carpet.

'Catherine?' Mammy lifted me by the elbow. 'What in God's name is the commotion? Would you ever stop messin', you're holding everyone up.'

'Mammy, the door's broken, the door ...'.

'Grandad will fix that when we get back. Come on with you. Jeez, we've missed the best of the day already. Like mobilising a blinkin' army getting you lot out the door. Jack!'

'But, Mam ...'.

Shepherded into the Fiesta ('Seatbelt, Catherine. Jack, would you ever stop waving that spade around? Jesus'), I watched in horror as Mammy locked the turquoise front door and got into the driver's seat. Beside me, Jack frowned over his Nintendo. Grandad unfolded a map of Inishowen on his knee, and began whistling 'The Mountains of Mourne' as Mammy drove down Glendermot Road towards the city.

The effect of Ebenezer's escape was immediate. I felt a jolt, like waking from a dream of falling. Derry seemed to gain altitude. The air thinned. Between the blue wrought-iron cross-hatch of Craigavon Bridge, a tank rolled past. Squat, determined, the thick green mast of its gun was pointed up towards the Fountain. My throat tightened. I wanted to loosen my seatbelt and shout for Mammy to turn back to Grandad's house to recapture Ebenezer, but I couldn't. My voice knotted in my throat, as in a nightmare of screaming.

As we drove out of Derry city, over the bombed-out, invisible border, past Bridge End's petrol stations, a reel of forgotten family memories looped before my eyes. I saw Granny Nora laughing, leaning on the backyard wall to gossip with the neighbours. I saw Dad's breath fogging in the cold docklands morning, and a dark figure stepping out of the alley in front of him. I saw five young soldiers gathered around a big gun at El Alamein. Over and over, the five young faces. Over and over, the still desert night. Over and over, the tug of momentum leading towards a terrible moment. And then nothing.

He slithered out. He flew out. He crawled out, using the last of his energy. In years to come, I would imagine all of these possibilities.

Ebenezer was heavy now, blanketed by the fumes of those unwanted memories. How could he help but belch out a couple of them as he edged towards the Foyle? And those memories lifted on the summer wind and flew back to their owners.

Regaining a memory is difficult. People kept aspects of their memories and fed Ebenezer the parts they couldn't bear. Mammy was able to cope with remembering Dad's face, but the memory of his laugh would have killed her. These were the things Ebenezer had kept hidden in Grandad's cupboard.

Cherished memories were harder to chew. They spiked like thistle flowers.

Stroke City. The City of Bones. Ebenezer had hidden in every house in this city at one time or another. The city on whose banks King James I landed. The city where the apprentice boys slammed the gates shut to prevent James's troops entering. Both sides claimed victory, one side calling it a barricade, the other calling it a siege. Either way, when the apprentice boys slammed shut those gates, a lot of other things in Derry got slammed shut too. A dog barks on a Bogside terrace. The bridge is cordoned off again. Another bomb threat. Another suspected arson attack. Whatever peace existed was because of the memories Ebenezer had kept in his belly for decades.

As he slid across the Foyle, two men on the river path were talking about the ceasefire. They spoke of Stormont. Decommissioning. Paisley. Adams. Good Friday. They didn't know that the memories that fuelled the conflict were not gone, only buried. And on the radio, they talked about 'stepping out of the shackles of history'.

'Come on, Cathy.' Jack tugged at my arm. 'Come on for a swim?'

'Go 'way, Jack.' I turned away from him, the bulge of a rainbow-striped windbreaker at my back. On the damp white sand of Doagh Island, a handful of families had set up colourful encampments, and the heads of a few swimmers bobbed in the surf. The sea air made everything tight, and beneath the cool stroke of the Atlantic I felt the prickle of a heat rash start to burn.

Hugging my knees, I closed my eyes and listened to Mammy and Grandad retelling memories they had told so often that I started to remember them myself. In my head I tried to copy their voices, to pepper my flat English accent with their Irish phrases: 'a clatter of wains', 'honest to God', 'a grand day altogether'. And I thought about Ebenezer. What was he doing now? Had he gone into the town? Had anyone seen him? Had he dragged the mottled scraps of my family's memories with him? And had he been taking other people's memories too?

Jack dived onto the sand in front of me again. 'C'mon, Cathy. C'mon, c'mon!'

'Okay, okay.' I got up, dusting sand from the seat of my swimsuit.

'Race ya!'

Jack took off towards the ocean, but the path to the water's edge was guarded by a fleet of sandworms. Marine insects had left tiny worm-shapes of sand dotted along the surf. Jack raced ahead, his sunken footprints deep in the wet grey sand, while I tiptoed gingerly around each gleaming sand turret, afraid there might be something inside the sand, some tiny, unseen danger. 'Come on, Cathy, ya scaredy-cat,' Jack laughed, 'they're only sandworms!' But I continued to step strategically until my pink toes reached the lapping mirror on which white clouds raced.

My brother howled at the clutch of the freezing Atlantic, and eventually I plunged after him, my skinny body cradled by the salty buoyancy. On the horizon, white horses danced. Jack lashed out into the waves, his pale arms chopping through them, while I paddled frantically, but never seemed to get any farther than the water around my face.

I didn't see the jellyfish either before or after it stung me in the centre of my palm, at the point where lines cross like barbed wire. And the gulls and the mountains and the big blue Atlantic had likely never heard anything like my wails.

Nearby children turned to stare as my sobs caused a rupture in the sunlight, a chink in the bright day.

When I ran back up the beach, Mammy dried my tears on the scratchy beach towel. And the day was bright, and Grandad was pouring cups of sandy tea. And later, as the sun fell behind the back of the Atlantic, I carried a bucket of shells I had carefully chosen, little pieces of Ireland I'd personally export across the Irish Sea.

The truth is, Ebenezer couldn't help it. Bitter memories were like seeds in his teeth. He couldn't help but spit out a few, and they bounced back to their owners, scattered across Ulster. Ebenezer slithered over the hill and up the town, and as soon as he reached Shipquay Street the cobbles rang with forgotten voices and boot-falls of the dead.

People paused in their tasks. They looked up, each stunned by a painful recollection long since shed. Some looked over their shoulders, suspecting a supernatural presence, not believing that the human mind could, by itself, conjure such nightmares.

Under archways and along the city walls, tension mounted towards boiling point like the steam inside Grandad's shrieking kettle. A noose tightened around the city until the air flattened. Detonated. All Ebenezer could do was crawl back, creep back to his cupboard.

It has always haunted me, but I wasn't to know. At the exact moment when I was crying over a jellyfish sting, a car bomb exploded over the border, taking thirty-one lives with it.

The news about Omagh didn't reach us until we were sitting around Grandad's television that evening. Grandad was nailing the cupboard door back into place when Mammy shouted, 'Daddy! God, come and see this. Christ.'

Grandad hobbled into the kitchen and stood beside her, staring at the TV. By then there were things written on their faces that I didn't—and, having been brought up in England, by definition couldn't—ever understand. I remember wanting to react, but not knowing how. And while I knew it was possible to envy someone their happiness, I would experience for the first time the aching loneliness of envying someone their grief.

It may well be an invented memory, but one of the details I recall from the evening after the Omagh bomb is my smiling Aunt Ruby arriving at Grandad's house with a bunch of pink geraniums. The flowers silenced the living room. A shocking, disrespectful cerise. Mammy took Aunt Ruby by the elbow and led her into the kitchen.

I remember everyone squished together on the brown sofa. Jack sitting on the floor, rolling a ping-pong ball over and over. Mammy was pouring the remainder of sandy tea from the beach flask into chipped *Royal Coronation* mugs. Grandad had made a watery soup by boiling diced carrots and onions with scraps of overcooked beef. The greasy bone-and-metal taste lingered on my tongue, like how I imagined the after-flavour of having chewed a thermometer. The unlit fire stared black in the grate, although it was cold enough to have lit it.

Slipping from my perch on the armrest, I snuck into the hall, clicking the door shut behind me. A bright square of sky sat in the small pane of glass on Grandad's turquoise front door. Dust floated in the gloomy photo negative of the empty hallway. Dropping to my knees on the rough carpet, I slipped my fingers under the cupboard door, which Grandad had fixed, in a fashion, by hammering it shut.

I waited for the icy head rush, the fantastic stream of light, but there was nothing. No auburn beehive. No still desert night. No polo-shirt buttons. No running shoes. Not one of the five young faces. Not even a heartbeat.

Palm still smarting from the sting of the unseen jellyfish, I withdrew my hand and cradled it to my chest. Shivering, I knelt in the wedge of light from the front door, until Grandad's voice inevitably said, 'Catherine?'

'Grandad … it's all my fault. I've been … I've been sneaking peaks at Ebenezer's memories coz I … I … I just wanted to see, but then the door broke and … and Ebenezer got loose, and now look what's happened in Omagh to all those people!'

My voice was swallowed by hot, cleansing tears, and Grandad lifted me to my feet.

He took my hand and pushed open the door of the good room, which we were only allowed to use if it was Christmas, or if someone had died. The tang of lavender polish greeted me, a scent of pressed flowers, as if the room were mummified. A gilt-framed photo of Granny Nora was propped proudly on the mantelpiece, its glass dustless. Grandad must have cleaned this room every day and then locked it again. This was another of his rituals.

'Love,' he said. 'Catherine, darlin'. Did I not tell you Ebenezer goes away off on holidays sometimes?'

'Yeah?' I hiccupped.

'Aye,' Grandad continued, 'sure he's away off, up to Magilligan Strand likely. But he'll be back, so he will. It wasn't you caused anything, darlin'.'

As I laid my head on Grandad's shoulder, I remember breathing in the polished good-room smell, listening to the sea-throb of traffic on Glendermot Road, and perhaps knowing that was to be my last encounter with Ebenezer and his cupboard full of half-chewed memories. That

Northern Ireland would no longer be confined to the TV. I'd soon begin to understand the phrase *Mixed Marriage* and the reason my parents had left. I'd finally realise the weight of the decision our parents had made when they moved to England; that opting out of the Troubles was never really an option, and that in the process of leaving, something undefinable had been lost.

They think my dad stumbled upon 'someone up to something' in the docklands that morning. It wasn't a political killing as such; more a chance; a misfortune; an incomplete memory. The details were never uncovered.

Last time I visited Ebenezer, I was grown. Grown and standing in the cement dust of the abandoned scullery, where the tall man behind me had just kicked the door in. 'How could they do this?' I said. 'What class of eejits bought Grandad's wee house and then left it to rot like this? Bastards.'

The Dublin man behind me was nervous. To Ebenezer, his nerves must have smelt like the sweat of rotting apples. He was nervous because it was his first time in Northern Ireland, because he loved me to death, and because at my request he had just kicked some stranger's door in. 'Come on, Cathy,' he said, 'we'd best not hang around. You've seen it now, love. No point in getting upset.'

Ignoring him, I knelt on the mouldy carpet and placed a hand on the cupboard door. Lines were worn into my palm now, and loneliness seeped from me. My copied accent had settled into a neutral lilt, and the confusion I'd felt as a child had only intensified. I'd moved to Dublin, but that hadn't solved anything. The older I'd become, the less Irish I felt, and also the less English, so that I now felt effectively stateless, lost between worlds.

I rubbed the cupboard door as if it were a dog's smooth head. Ever since Grandad passed away, Ebenezer had been in there sleeping, sneaking out occasionally to scour the city, hunting down its most hurtful memories and syphoning them off, bringing them back to the cupboard and sucking them like carbolic lozenges until they dissolved into nothing.

Ebenezer had missed me. As a gift, he breathed a memory back to me through the keyhole. It wasn't something I would notice immediately (gaining a happy memory has a less noticeable effect than losing one), but it would be some comfort. Weeks later I discovered this memory on a cold winter's day. Walking down a Dublin street, I was suddenly arrested by the scent of a real coal fire. And I pictured Grandad kneeling by Ebenezer's cupboard and slowly feeding his newspapers, and his memories, into the dark.

How to be a Billionaire

It's too bad Shanika walks past my desk just when I've got my hand in my mouth, messing with the tooth that's bothering me. Shanika's got freckles on her nose and she's got hair like autumn. She's the only kid in our class that's Irish, apart from Felix, who says he's from Cork, but I know he's Nigerian like me. My brother Ezekiel always says Forget It Kingsley, Shanika's never gonna fancy you. But one time when we were washing our hands after doing Art, Shanika's hand touched mine, and I felt sort of funny, and ever since then I've just known I like her and nothing can stop it.

Tugging at my back tooth, think it's coming loose. Shanika sees my sloppy hand and the toddler-slobber on my chin. She looks away quick, like she's pretending she's not looking. Larissa whispers something to her, and they do those girl sniggers that make you feel awful. I put my hood up, even though the school rule is *No Hoods Up In Class*.

Right then, Fourth Class, Mr O'Neill says, take out your Gaeilge. But I don't bother, coz there's no point when I don't understand nothing. Only Irish I know is *Law Va Soo Ass*. That means *Hands Up*, but I don't never put my hand up, coz I don't never know none of the answers. So I put my head down on the table. Time for a snooze.

Kingsley…? Kingsley… are you ready?

Miss Lacey's standing in the doorway, looking confused like always. She's got brown hair that she ties back, and glasses that are always falling off, and she says *Call Me Sarah*, but I never do. Mr O'Neill comes over and speaks with Miss Lacey, and I hear my name. Kingsley … no lunch … homework not done … and somethin somethin somethin … Then Miss Lacey looks at me and says Right Then Kingsley, *Off We Go*. As I stroll over to the door, I pass Shanika sharpening pencils by the bin. Wonder what she's thinking about. Please Lord she's thinking about me. Then I follow Miss Lacey down the hall.

Miss Lacey's my Learning Support Teacher. Nobody tells me how come she takes me out of class to her small room, where I have to read and write and do maths stuff. I think it's coz they say I've got Special Needs, and I need Time Out coz sometimes people piss me off, and sometimes I can't do stuff. I'm ten but I'm still in Fourth Class coz I had to repeat Junior Infants, coz I was so crap they made me do it *Twice*.

So I come into Miss Lacey's classroom and I'm still messing with my tooth, circle it and sorta nudge it with my tongue. What are you doing Kingsley? Miss Lacey asks.

I'm pulling out my tooth.

WHAT? She's proper shocked like. Kingsley, stop that.

Stop what? I'm not doing nothing.

Kingsley take your hand out of your mouth, or else I'm taking you back to Mr O'Neill.

Ok, Ok, Ok, I say to her. Jeezus … take it easy. I open my mouth wide. Can you see that? I ask her. Can you see my wobbly tooth?

Miss Lacey looks in my mouth, but not proper closely. Is that a baby tooth, she asks, or a big tooth?

Dunno.

You have to mind your big teeth, Kingsley, coz if they fall out you can't get any more.

You can, I tell her. Some people sells their teeth, I saw it on the net. So you can buy another teeth.

Miss Lacey looks at me, confused. No Kingsley, when you get a fake tooth it's not actually someone else's tooth. It's made out of porcelain and it costs a lot of money.

How much? I ask.

Oh gosh … about one thousand euro.

What's *Por-See-Lin*?

Miss Lacey takes a cup from her desk. The cup's red and white spotty and it says *Thank You Teacher* and it's had coffee in it coz you can smell it. This is porcelain, Miss Lacey taps the cup with her finger nails. See? They make the crowns— the false teeth—out of this material. Miss Lacey's happy now. She likes it when she's explaining about stuff.

Right, I say, so they get a cup, smash it, and make a tooth?

Now Miss Lacey's had enough talking and she says Right Mister Kingsley, it's time for *you* to do some reading.

In the yard at Small Break, my tongue is still playing with that tooth. How come they make fake tooths out of *Pore-See-Lin*? And how come that stuff costs so much, when cups don't cost a thousand euro? Imagine how many teeth you could make out of one teacup. Imagine if I took all my mam's teacups and sold them to a guy who was making fake teeth, and he said *Thanks Very Much Partner* and gave me a thousand euro per cup. I'd go straight over to Shanika's house and tell her *guess what Shanika, I'm a billionaire …*

and then *SLAM!* Something hits the back of my head. I spin around, fast. It's Marcel with that stupid goofy smile on his face.

Marcel is not that smart. I think in our class the most smartest one is Anna and the second smartest one is Patryk and the least smartest one is Marcel. He's Romanian and he's got brown hair that sticks up, and the only good thing about him is that he has a moustache and no one else has one. Mr O'Neill always says *Why are you late Marcel? ... Where's your homework Marcel? ... Marcel!!! Less Of The Attitude!* But Marcel just sits there, watching Teacher like he's watching the TV.

So anyway, Marcels just punched me. What you do that for? I say.

Coz Shanika says you're gay, douchebag.

Well that's it. I land him some punches. But I don't hardly even get stuck in when hands are pulling us off each other. I didn't even hardly get started!

So then I'm marched to the Principal's Office. She's a small woman about the same height as our granny in Nigeria, except that Granny's warm and round and wears bright coloured clothes so she always looks like a mango or a tangerine. The Principal's got grey hair and a greyish kind of face and always wears black. She's even got bones sticking out on her wrists, and I want to ask her how come she's got them bones sticking out like that.

Kingsley, Principal says, I'm very disappointed.

Yeah, I say.

Principal says *Pardon?*

So I say louder YEAH!

Oh Lord she looks like she's going to reach across the table and put those bony white hands around my neck. So that's detention for me, and a letter home. But my mam don't even care about no letter, and my dad's in Nigeria now, and my sister Faith has gone off to live in Galway, like she always said she would. My sister used to be the boss. One time when we lived in town, we were having dinner and some guys shouted through the letterbox GO BACK TO AFRICA! Well Faith just slammed her knife and fork down and shouted back WE'RE NOT FROM AFRICA! WE'RE FROM THE NAVAN ROAD! Nobody would mess with Faith. But now it's just me, Mam and Ezekiel. No boss in sight.

After break, Mr O'Neill pulls on his jacket and picks up his silver travel mug. Right then, guys. I've to take the cricket team to their match. Mrs Boyle's teaching you till lunch. Best behaviour, right?

We all sort of mumble something and Mrs Boyle walks in, Morning Boys and Girls. She's wearing some posh kinda dress thing and her nails go swish-swish across the interactive whiteboard. Today Boys and Girls we're learning how to write a personal narrative.

Ezekiel thuds his head onto the desk. Larissa whispers something in Lithuanian that sends Rasmus and Patryk into stitches.

Mrs Boyle gives a smile like a razor. Boys and Girls. Attention Please. This is my example. And she shows this thing she's typed on the interactive whiteboard about where she's from in Ros Co Mon, and it was a big house on a farm with rambling hills. Anyone know what *Rambling* means? she asks, but nobody in our class knows. And they had apple trees they climbed, she says, and a big kitchen where her mam baked cakes and the family ate dinner and spoke Irish coz they liked it or something. Then she says Now Boys and Girls, I want you to write about where you're from.

I don't know what to write. Where I'm from on Hunter's Run is a block of flats that's not finished. The stairs are filled with flyers saying *Buy One Get One Free, Sky TV, Macari's Takeaway*. There's a lift that's normally broke. Behind the flats there's this place everyone calls Wasteland. It's where more flats were going to be, but I guess they never finished it, so now it's just mud and bits of bricks and weeds and long grass and bits of stuff like somebody's door or somebody's window.

The only cool thing is Wasteland's got these big old metal huts the builders left behind. Sometimes Ezekiel and me go and sit on top of the huts and they make banging noises, and it's awesome and high up there. People put graffiti on the sides of the huts so they're always nice and colourful. One time we saw two teenagers near one of the huts and Ezekiel said they had just been *Having Sex*, and one other time we found a condom in the Wasteland too. I thought it looked sort of squishy and not like something you'd want to put your *you-know-what* into. Another time when we were sitting on the huts we had a smoke of a cigarette I'd nicked from Dad, but I didn't like it much.

All the other kids in the class are writing, but I don't know what to write. I wonder what Shanika's writing about. Bet she's writing something real good. There's nothing to write where I'm from. No fields or apple trees or big farm kitchens or cakes or Rambling Hills or nothing. So I just sit for a while, and then I start drawing my name graffiti-style like the writing on those big metal huts. It's going good and I'm working on the 'g' when Mrs Boyle behind me says *Kingsley What's This?* She lifts my book by the corner, like it's a baby's shitty nappy. Is this a true reflection of where you're from Kingsley?

Yeah, I say.

Marcels sniggering. I'd like to punch him again but too bad Miss Lacey's in the doorway. Time to go.

Kingsley, Miss Lacey says, Sit up … Kingsley you're not even concentrating.

I've got the pencil in my hand and she's making me do Page 3 of this book of handwriting exercises for Junior Infants. Only good thing is at least Shanika's not here seeing me doing this baby stuff. Why are you not even trying today Kingsley? Miss Lacey says. If you do this page of this handwriting then we'll do *Finding Out Stuff* on the net, and then we'll go back to class. She looks at her watch. She's got that worried line on her head like always. Come on Kingsley, she says. We've only got half an hour.

Stop Naggin Me! I say. Why you always naggin me?

I don't nag you Kingsley, when do I ever nag you?

You naggin me right now!

Then she goes quiet.

Things were better when I had a Special Needs Sistant called Cathy. She was good. She always helped me do stuff, but she helped me real sneaky like, so nobody knew she was helping me. If some kid started pisstaking me, Cathy said pass me your work this second! and then she'd find some mistake in that kid's work, and then she'd Give Out Buckets, and then that kid would stop pisstaking me for sure.

Last year Cathy said she couldn't help me no more coz she was losing her job. I asked How Come and Cathy said *Gov-Ment Cut Backs* and her face went red like she was gonna cry. To be honest, I'm not totally sure what *Gov-Ment* does, but I know it's some old guys in suits who like cutting things. Maybe they're barbers or maybe they're grasscutters. But why did they have to cut back Cathy? One time when I didn't have no lunch, Cathy bought me a sausage roll and it was good and flaky and Cathy said *You*

Messy Wee Thing and we both laughed and laughed and I felt sort of happy.

After school Ezekiel and me go to this Blanch Kids Klub thing, and its crap coz the only thing we do is make Christmas cards when it's not even Christmas, it's like November or something, and play games and listen to people from the Red Cross talking about what to do in an *Ee Mer Gen See*. The only good thing is when they take us somewhere on the minibus, like today they're taking us to Phoenix Park.

Let's Play Rounders the Volunteers say. I don't want to Play Rounders, so I just lay back on the grass, like I'm a billionaire and this is my garden, mine and Shanika's, and all the other people are paying to be here. I can hear the other kids shouting, and the bat hitting the ball, and far away traffic, and I guess I just doze off.

When I wake I feel rusty like I've been sleeping for years. Good nap Kingsley? One of them *Vo-Lun-Teers* is handing me a plastic cup of orange juice. Kidz Klub never have anything good like Coke or Fanta or Sprite. Hey hey, the Volunteer says, you've got to sit up to drink it Kingsley else you'll choke. So I sit up, glug the juice and look over the park.

First I just look. And then I say … oh! Oh … coz it's Miss Lacey *Call Me Sarah*. And she's walking across the grass with some tall black dude's arm around her, and you don't even notice he's black and she's white, you just notice they're so happy. Teacher's not frowning. She's wearing jeans and her hair loose and she's laughing and the tall black guy's laughing too, like they just discovered the most secretest and most funniest thing in the universe and only they know about it. Miss Lacey doesn't see me, coz the yellow grass is tall over my head … even after they've gone I can still sort of see them, like after someone takes a photo with flash and it stays on the backs of your eyelids.

That's when I have the idea. I'm gonna ask Shanika out.

First it was easy peasy lemon squeezy. Get Ezekiel to do it. All the girls like my brother. Even Anna with the long blonde plaits, and Hope who's South African and even wears a bra. Even she likes Ezekiel. Simple, get Ezekiel to ask Shanika and Larissa to hang out at our place. So, next Monday in school I ask Ezekiel to ask them, and first he says *No Way Kingsley Man … Are You Crazy?* but then I go in Mam's purse and get a tenner and give it to him and then he says *Yes*.

So next Friday after school Shanika and Larissa meet us at the roundabout and we walk over to our place to hang out at the Wasteland. My heart starts speeding up pretty fast when I see Shanika in her pale blue jeans, white T-shirt and pink hoody. But Ezekiel just walks up to the girls and says hey, what's the story? As if hanging out with girls is something normal that happens every day. Larissa giggles, messes with her earring and looks weird at Ezekiel. Then Ezekiel and Larissa stroll off, and me and Shanika just stand there looking at each other. Shanika looks so good and clean. I can't think of nothing to say to her coz she looks so perfect.

Hey Shanika, I say, you wanna see something really cool? Climb up here on the hut with me and we'll see the Rambling Hills.

Shanika doesn't look too sure about the idea, but I think she's impressed coz I said the word *Rambling*. She laughs. You're so funny Kingsley.

So I climb up the side of the hut and then I grab Shanika's hand to help her up and *Oh Lord, I'm holding Shanika's hand!* I nearly drop her, thinking about that. So I sit down on the hut and Shanika sits too and it's just us on our own in the big blue sky. I say It's cool huh?

Shanika says Yeah, but I can tell she's worried her jeans are getting dirty, coz to be honest even I'm worried about that.

Did you know Shanika, I shuffle a little closer, fake tooths are made out of *Pore-See-Lin*.

Oh really? Shanika looks at me close. First time I realise those freckles on her nose are caramel colour, like the middle of a Mars bar, and her eyes are green, but in the middle they're orange like traffic lights when they're waiting to change.

Yeah, I say, and fake tooths cost thousands of euro, and *Por-See-Lin* comes from cups. So imagine you had some cups, you could make hundreds of tooths and sell them and be a billionaire.

Really? Shanika starts playing with her hair, twisting it round and round her finger. Being close to Shanika like this makes my breathing sort of funny, like I'm in space and I'm running out of *Ox-E-Gen*.

You know Shanika, I move a little closer, if an astronaut gets one small hole in his space suit, he can get crushed by *Gra-Vee-Tee* and then he can hexplode?

Uh-huh? Shanika says. We're really close now and her skin smells like chips and strawberry gum. I put my hand on Shanika's hand and she jumps a little, like she's just been stung. Shanika looks at me funny now. Then she looks over her shoulder really quickly, like she's only just realised we're *On Our Own*.

Maybe we should go find Larrissa and Ezekiel, Shanika says. She takes her hand out of my hand and she gets up carefully and rubs down her jeans. The fake tooth thing's not working, and the hexploding astronauts is not working. My heart its thumping coz I know this is my last chance with Shanika. I've got to try a new tactic. Fast. So I leap down off the metal shed and I sort of pull Shanika down with me. I land ok, but Shanika lands sort of sorely with her leg kind of twisted.

It's too bad that Shanika is still on the ground when Ezekiel and Larissa come round the corner arm in arm. After that there's a lot of girl screaming and shouting and Ezekiel with his hands on his head shouting *Kingsley! What The Fuck?!* and I go running back over the Wasteland. I race over the part where they didn't finish building. I jump over the place where we once saw a dead rat, coz I won't never step on there. Along the road where Polish kids have drawn pictures of suns and moons and flowers with pink chalk on the black road. I leg it up all those stairs, coz the lift is broken. Into my flat and lock the door. And I dunno why I've got water on my face, it's like I'm crying or something. Mam's asleep in the bed. She's working tonight.

Monday morning in school, Ezekiel doesn't look at me. He's been ignoring me all weekend and didn't even want to play football or nothing. Shanika and Larissa aren't here. Everything's quiet. Mr O'Neill says, Right Fourth Class, take out your Gaeilge.

I still feel sort of strange since Friday and my heart's still booming. Where's Shanika? What's she thinking? I feel sorta sick, so I decide I need to do some graffiti. I lean over the desk and swipe Marcel's pencil case of felt tips and hide it in the pocket of my hoody. Marcel looks pissed off, but he can't do nothing coz after our fight in the yard he's on his *Last Chance*, and so am I. Marcel's felt tips are perfect for doing a new graffiti name, like the one Mrs Boyle robbed off me, but I'm only starting the letter K when I hear my name.

Kingsley. And the Principal's stood behind me, like she's been stood there for millions of years. She's not smiling. Not at all. Come this way Kingsley, she says.

So I'm in the Principal's office. Again. And she's frowning at me and she's saying Big disappointment Kingsley, big disappointment. And I think *Tell Me About It*. I've never felt so disappointed in my life as when I realised that Shanika don't fancy me. Stealing ... Principal says. Recklessness ... she says. Sexual Harassment ... she says, and I feel my cheeks burning, bit embarrassed to be honest coz the Principal just said the word *Sex*. Letting down the school and the family and the community, she says. Not a good reflection on yourself. On the school. On the family. On the community.

Yeah, I say. That tooth is still bothering me. I try to wriggle it with my tongue.

Kingsley, she says. This Is Serious.

Then there's a knock knock on Principal's door. It's Mrs Burke the secretary. Sorry, she says to the Principal, can I have a word?

Principal says Wait Here Kingsley, and she goes out and shuts the door behind her.

Her office is full of paper. Piles of paper on the desk. On the computer. On the floor. Why does she need so much paper? I pick a few papers up. Throw them and they fall down like white birds. There's lots of grey drawers. I try them but they're locked. On the wall there's photos. Classes of kids. I spot our class from First Class. There's Patryk, Anna and Jakob, their hair so blonde it's nearly white. There's Marcel looking like he pissed himself coz he didn't speak no English. There's me with my Ireland T-shirt that I refused to take off me for one week. There's Shanika with pigtails and a flowery dress and those gorgeous Mars bar freckles on her nose. There's Hussam and

Hameed and Hamza and Adeola and Precious and Ayodele. There's Ezekiel's face shining. We looked good I think.

Then I look up. Above the kids photos there's the teachers photo. They're wearing their best clothes and smiling like they just saved the world or something. The teachers look a bit pale, I think, so I take Marcel's pencilcase from the front pocket of my hoody.

Afterwards they all said *How Did He Have The Time To Do It When The Principal Was Only Gone For Three Minutes?* But really you know, I'm quick at colouring in. When you're a Special Needs kid like me, colouring in is all you get to do. I'm the Usain Bolt of colouring in. It took me about two minutes. First I coloured the teachers' faces brown, dark brown and yellow. Then I got excited and I coloured a few more of them pink, red, green, blue. I coloured the Principal in the Ireland colours. White stripe on her nose. I laughed. That's funny. Then I stopped colouring. I put the photo back in the cardboard frame, and put the frame back on the wall.

The Principal told Mam that I've got Anger Issues, but I wasn't angry at that moment. I was pretty happy, looking at all those colourful teachers and all those smiling kids underneath. I could have looked at that all day.

When Miss Lacey comes over to see me, she brings me some Match Cards. She sorta sneaks them in under her jacket coz I think teachers aren't meant to bring presents to people who are *Sus-Pen-Dead*. I don't know if you collect these Kingsley, she says. I look at them and nod, don't say nothing coz I'm still thinking about Shanika and feeling sort of bad. I brought you this book too, Miss Lacey says, it's called *Amazing Facts About Our Planet!* I nod and take it. She frowns, worried looking. I want to ask her if she's still walking around Phoenix Park with that tall black dude. But her face don't give no clues.

You've been Let Down by the Sis-Tem Kingsley, Miss Lacey says, but I dunno if she's really talking to me or not, coz she looks sort of *Up Set*. You need more support, and so does your mam, she says. She looks at me really serious now, Kingsley … I'm sorry about what happened. I know you're better than that, Ok?

Ok … I say and then I say Oh! What do you know? My wobbly tooth just came out!

I spit it out in my hand and it's covered in blood and spit, and Miss Lacey says Oh Dear God, and I laugh. Finally! Tonight I know I'm going to sleep like a baby with that new clean gap in my gums. And you've got to be careful to clean your gums, coz gum disease is a killer. I know, coz I saw it on the net. Maybe next time I see Shanika I'll tell her about gum disease and she'll be dead impressed. She'll put her arm in my arm and we'll go walking like Miss Lacey and that black dude in the park. And it'll be worth all the fights and all the trips to the Principal's office and worth being held back in Junior Infants and having a dad that's gone away to Lagos, and a sister that's gone off to Galway, and a brother that's smarter than me and all the other kids laughing at me and worth even being *Sus Pen Ded* and everything, just to be in that moment.

Infinite Landscapes

'Abeyomi had always known I wasn't destined to stay in this world,' the young Simidele wrote on the back of a cereal box in looping purple ink. Even as a child, Simi was in the habit of noting down her experiences, never suspecting that thirty years later I would use her box of scraps to piece together the legend of my origins. Simi's writings, along with Abeyomi's memories and the cuttings I have pasted in my scrapbook over the years, have allowed me to reconstruct a narrative of sorts. And when friends ask why I waste so much time trying to put together Simi's story, my usual response is to shrug and tell them, 'If you don't know your roots, then you can't understand where you're coming from.'

Abeyomi was my grandmother. She was a proud Yoruba woman with a high forehead and an obsession with the music of The Chieftains. Memories of her evoke the caramelised fragrance of frying plantains, the ripple of Irish reels from the kitchen and the tropical flowers of her *gele* headwraps. She left Nigeria for Ireland in her early twenties and started work as a nurse at St James's Hospital. There she met my grandad, Cathal O'Doherty, a plumber from Dún Laoghaire, who landed in at A&E one morning with his left leg scalded from a boiler incident. 'He'd the cheek of the divil,' my grandmother told me. 'There he was, in a right state, blisters all over, but that didn't stop him from asking me out to a dance.' My grandparents married soon after, settled on Tivoli Avenue and started planning a family.

Years of heartache followed. Time after time they visited the Early Pregnancy Unit at the Rotunda. Time after time the monitor showed nothing but darkness floating around inside Abeyomi's womb, the watery oblong of a pregnancy sack with nothing inside it. There were always the same words of consolation, '*Not to worry, love; you'll have another one soon.... You'll be back in here before Christmas.*' The same room in the Rotunda, reserved for moments of shock, disappointment, grief. The same cups of milky tea. And then the long drive home to Dún Laoghaire, silence gathering between them like the stillness before snowfall.

This cyclical pattern was eventually shattered when my grandmother came home one winter evening, slammed the door behind her and shouted, 'Cathal! We have a heartbeat!' Her hands trembled as she told him about the scan she'd had. The pregnancy she'd kept secret. Elated, the couple splashed out and ordered Domino's pizza for dinner. But later, once they'd settled on the sofa for the evening, Abeyomi pressed pause on the remote and put her hand on Cathal's knee. 'Love,' she said, 'this won't be a normal baby.'

On-screen, a blonde girl was paused open-mouthed in her soaring rendition of 'Wind Beneath My Wings'. Cathal took his wife's hand and gave it a squeeze. 'What do you mean, "not normal", love? I've always said I'd love any child that we …'.

'No.' Her black eyes watered into inky pools. 'This child will be *abiku*.'

'It'll be what?'

37

'Cursed,' she hiccupped, 'a child of the spirits.'

Cathal kissed her forehead. 'Ach, love, that's just quaint old superstitions so it is.'

Just then the TV unpaused itself, and the blonde girl soared into her chorus, '*Did you ever know that you're my heeeee-roooooo?*'

Tutting, as if the singer had offended her personally, Abeyomi re-paused the telly and threw the remote down so hard that the battery fell out and rolled under the sofa. She folded her arms across her chest. 'Cathal, there is *nothing* quaint about a spirit child.'

Abeyomi was forty-three at that time. She had lived in Ireland for more than half her life, but still held on to her Yoruban beliefs. Whether her baby had been conceived beside the Liffey or in Lagos did not make any difference to my spirited grandmother. Among Yoruba it was considered serious bad luck for a child to take up residence in the belly of a woman who had lost so many other children before. So, that night, Abeyomi called her mother, Sama Nanosi, on Skype. The wise woman of Kwara crouched over a cola, her dreadlocks brushing against the webcam as she listened to her daughter's story.

'Mark my words,' Sama Nanosi nodded, 'this child will be *abiku*. A spirit child predestined to forever come and go.'

Abeyomi came off Skype with a list of tricks and remedies. From that night on she began leaving a pair of open scissors by her bedside to scare the spirits away. 'Don't be daft, love,' Cathal said. 'Sure the doctor said everything's grand. There's no need for all this fuss.' Abeyomi ignored him and polished the scissor blades, her mouth set in a determined line. Sighing, my grandfather left her to it. He busied himself by decorating the spare bedroom with rainbow wallpaper, while in Abeyomi's belly the child grew stronger.

And on the day newborn Simidele O'Doherty first opened her shocking green eyes in the Rotunda Hospital, my grandmother's suspicions were sadly confirmed. Little Simi burst into life shuddering and wailing from the scars of past lives barely lived, and suffering withdrawal symptoms from the spirit kingdom she had left behind. As Abeyomi had dreaded, through her umbilical cord Simi had absorbed the spirits of all the other lost babies gone before. Simi would never settle in the skin of one personality, but would always be moving, changing from one soul to another. She was fated to be seduced and misguided by the spirits, to read minds and skip between dimensions and to be eternally distrusted in a world that fears the unfamiliar.

Concerned for the fate of their newest family member, the Yoruban side of Simi's family tried all they could think of to chase the *abiku* spirit away from her. Abeyomi and Cathal's terraced house on Tivoli Avenue received a constant flow of calls and emails from aunts and cousins in Kwara and Oyo bearing advice and remedies. 'Keep away from iroko, baobab and silk cotton trees,' a cousin in Kwara advised, becoming offended when Abeyomi pointed out that these trees do not exist in Ireland. Sama Nanosi suggested they should avoid trees altogether, for these were the seating places of spirits. 'Stay out of bright sunlight,' an aunt from Oyo told them, 'and no crying over the child. Each tear you cry she will convert for diamonds in the spirit kingdom.'

Kneeling by Simi's bedside, Abeyomi turned to her Gods. 'Leave her be,' she implored Olofi, the conduit between heaven and earth. 'Let her stay,' she begged the supreme god, Eledumare. 'Give her the spark of life, Ayé. Allow my daughter to stay.' And each afternoon she wheeled Simi's pram around Dún Laoghaire in relentless circles while she tried to discover where the child had hidden her spirit key, an object whose discovery would convince their daughter to stay.

But all the incantations to Eledumare, the late-night vigils and the open scissors left by the child's bedside were to no avail. Each morning Simi's green eyes would carry glints of the electric dreams from which she'd woken, and it was clear as day to anyone present that Simidele O'Doherty was as much an *abiku* child as ever.

Growing up, I often heard stories of how Simi's youngest years were spent tousling among the spirits, who delighted in playing mind games with the humans. Simi's earliest drawings show the spirits as shapes of colourful light lingering around her. A recurring image shows a spirit in the shape of a cat, its bluish tail curled around Simi's leg, its red eyes flashing. Other pictures show spirits of Abeyomi's dead babies as soft pink cloud shapes scampering after Simi across the floorboards. 'Sometimes we'd see a shadow dashing across the bathroom wall,' my Granny told me, 'or we'd hear a buzz, like the frantic flutter of a trapped night moth. Other times, I'd step into a patch of warm light and I'd know there was something there. Not quite living. Not quite dead. *Something.*'

Some of my grandparents' tales of spirit mischief have been retold so often that they have worked their way into my memory. I now imagine I was there to witness the events myself. My favourite story is of how Abeyomi lulled the downy-haired Simi to sleep in her cot one day, only to find her dozing in the unlit oven a few minutes later, her face grimy from oven grease, smelling of last night's chicken burgers, the back of her head marked by the oven shelf. Then there's the story of how Cathal locked the front door one night only to find it wide open the next morning. He still describes the eerie stillness, the soft sea brume seeping around the door frame. Nothing had been stolen, but a strange sadness had crept into the house like a sea fret.

'Honest to God, I was almost beginning to believe your granny's stories,' my grandfather told me. He was reminded of whispers he'd heard as a wain of changelings and fairy forts. And he began to view Simidele as a volatile and potentially dangerous gift.

To an outsider, Simi's antics might have seemed like normal toddler tantrums. Playing chase with the dead babies, Simi would often toddle along with her arms crossed behind her back to prevent anyone from holding her hand. Set on a headlong track like this, without her chubby arms to balance her, she would often fall. She'd sit and wail, then she'd pick herself up and start running again. No one but her parents would have suspected there were ghosts and lost children chasing after her.

'Simi's imagination is just wonderful,' a second class teacher at Scoil Mhúire beamed at the O'Dohertys as she slid the child's copybook across the desk between them. In front of Cathal and Abeyomi, a diary entry in Simi's loopy handwriting was illustrated with pictures of pink and turquoise spirits dancing the limbo in the sand.

'On Saterday we went to the beech and I said Daddy can the spirits com in the car and daddy said no they fuking can't and then the spirits got angree and playd in daddys enjin and then daddys enjin wouldn't start daddy said forfuksake and then he fix it and then the spirit babees playd wid me outsid and then we sleept.'

'Simi's an imaginative child,' Cathal laughed nervously.

'Incredible,' the primrose-bloused teacher gushed.

Throughout Simi's childhood, Abeyomi and Cathal worried that her strange behaviour would make her a target for school bullies. 'I spent my life fearing she'd be picked on,' my grandmother told me. But she need not have been so concerned. Although Simi frequently displayed unexplainable knowledge about strangers' personal lives, people tended to attribute this to lucky guesses, never noticing that Simi was psychic. Alternative lifestyle trends ensured that when Simi spent two days up a sycamore in Phoenix Park, or turned up at Scoil Mhuire with her hair bright blue, people presumed she was simply being hip. No one would have guessed that the spirits had tied her to the sycamore with thistle strings as a forfeit for a lost bet, or that the lost spirit babies had puked in her hair until it turned blue.

At worst, my grandmother told me with a sigh, Simi's peculiar abilities led people to make incorrect assumptions about her. Strangers often assumed that Simi was a generous and considerate person, which, apart from the odd moment of hormone-induced benevolence, she was not. When Simi enquired after a stranger's dying grandmother, or warned a classmate about an impending personal catastrophe, people presumed that the alluring green-eyed girl was being kind, but in such cases Simi was just showing off.

Reading between the lines of Abeyomi's stories, I imagine that Simi's personality was that of someone whose parents had spent the first twelve years of her life enticing her to stay. Whenever Simi caught a cold, or fell over in the yard, Abeyomi feared the worst. The cold would develop into pneumonia. The scraped knees would turn septic. The bumped head would clot into a concussion. And yet, Simi continued to stay. On the back of a free Dublin postcard, she wrote, 'It's like swinging in a hammock between worlds. Surrounded by the spirits of deceased relatives and future generations. Soothed by the tug of both past and future.'

In her mid teens, Simi began to create collages by sticking bits of broken teabags and nettle leaves onto paper plates and smearing these with colourful inks. Her Leaving Cert art exhibition was unlike anything the school had ever seen. By the age of eighteen, Simi's creative brazenness secured her a place at Dún Laoghaire College of Art and Design. On Simi's epic canvases, spirits crawled and coiled around bystanders' heads. In her most impressive piece, burnt toast, used condoms and nail clippings depicted a naked woman strapped to a plantain tree whilst playing an Irish harp.

'Simidele O'Doherty's intercultural narratives reflect a vibrant new era of Irish Modern Art,' one of the *Irish Times* articles in my scrapbook claims. 'What O'Doherty achieves in her work is to open a dialectic between the local and the international by interposing traditional Neolithic symbolism with Yoruban oral traditions.'

Within months of graduation, Simi's striking 'spirit collages' were highly sought-after. But Simi's paintings puzzled and divided the critics. In an infamous TV interview for *Modern Art Now*, the art critic Ben Dawson asked her, 'Do you find the complex duality of your Nigerian and Irish identities to be the cause of a necessary aesthetic clash in your work?'

'No,' Simi replied, 'but I find your question to be bleedin' annoying.'

Such interviews soon garnered Simi a reputation as one of Ireland's most obnoxious artists. Sales of her paintings soared, enabling her to earn a modest living and to rent a small studio overlooking Dún Laoghaire harbour.

Simi's diary describes how, on a damp December evening when she was twenty-five, she walked into the Sea Bar on the quayside at Dún Laoghaire. She knew instantly that the barmaid was two-and-a-half days pregnant. That the fat couple sitting by the window would shag in seven different positions that night. That the old man at the bar would break his wrist next Tuesday, and that the friend he was talking to had cancerous cells mutating in the backs of his eyelids. But when she turned her attention to a man sitting alone at a table in the corner of the pub, his aura was a black hole that offered no glimpse of the past or the future.

Frustrated, Simi glared at the man until he was socially obliged to walk over to her and ask in a polite BBC accent, 'Sorry, do I know you from somewhere?'

'No,' Simi replied. But she allowed the man to buy her a pint and stare at her, while she tried unapologetically to force entry into his past and burgle his future.

'Could I perhaps have your number?' the Englishman asked.

'Guess it,' Simi replied.

From the start of their relationship, the Englishman must have had doubts about Simi's temperament. I suppose it took a middle-aged chartered accountant not to notice the glint in Simi's eyes. And the way she slipped out of bed at night to tiptoe naked in search of the spirits, who whistled to her from behind the double-glazing of the man's semi-detached home. Abeyomi and Cathal encouraged this relationship, openly relieved that their daughter's spirit was finally being tamed by the attention of this grey-suited businessman from Sussex.

Simi married the Englishman on an August day that smelt of rain, and for a short time things seemed normal. In one diary entry, Simi describes how the spirits retreated in a huff to the slopes of the Sugar Loaf Mountain, and the spirit babies, starved of attention, started wasting away. Around this time she stopped painting sadistic spirit orgies and started painting insipid still-lives, which didn't sell. Her diary entries thin out at this point and become grocery lists. 'Peas, fairy liquid, toilet roll, marshmallows.... To do: hoover kitchen, phone dentist, unblock shower in en suite.'

Futile as it is to reimagine the past, I've often amused myself by wondering how things might have turned out if Simi's life had remained poised in that fragile equilibrium. This story might have unfolded differently had it not been for one late summer evening two and a half years later, when Simi was walking along the Harbour Road at Dún Laoghaire and saw a tall black man leaning against a wall waiting for her.

In one of her diary entries, Simi describes how 'daylight was fading, and the wet grey road snaked into the distance. A sharp sea breeze gathered itself up into a crescendo as I crossed over the road and into the man's smile.'

'Good evening ...' the stranger said. He took her hand, and Simi knew right then that she had been found. Located. Pinpointed with GPS. It was if she were an unnamed comet, whose trajectory had suddenly been plotted across a dark and empty sky, mapping her way forward. The man was an *abiku* too, and Simi recognised him as such because he smelt of congealed spirit baby puke, and he was able to study her very intently without ever looking at her face. He said he was from a small republic with no name, and that his name meant 'hope' in a language no one could understand. 'I've been waiting for you for a thousand years,' he told Simi.

'I know that,' she replied.

Unfettered by the chains of human caution or obligation, Simi fell headlong into this new love. And for a brief chink in time they were an island. A two-person planet. Meeting always at the harbour wall, or in the park's lush seascape. These infinite landscapes the *abiku* man craved. He told Simi stories of a landlocked republic, mischievous goats, lackadaisical goat-boys, praise poetry and a people praying for rain. 'In my country, spirit children are worshipped,' he told her. 'That's why I'm going back there. I never felt so shamed and belittled as I have felt here.'

'I'll come with you so,' Simi told him, but he shook his head.

'Let's face it. There's nothing for you in my country, Simidele. For your sake I would stay, but I can't live like this.'

'For feck's sake, take me with you!'

'Simi, you wouldn't be happy in my country … and Ireland doesn't hold much for me.'

'You stupid eejit!' Simi screamed. 'You know we'll both be bleedin' tortured!'

The *abiku* man laughed and stroked her cheek, and Simi knew right then that their joint fates were sealed. They were destined to hunger after each other throughout all eternity, as after an enticing mirage that melts into the glare of a summer road.

'But why the hell did he have to leave?' I once asked Abeyomi.

My wise grandmother stroked my hair. 'I don't know, pet. I guess sometimes, in love, the wrong decisions are made for all the right reasons.'

'The *abiku* man told me time would heal,' Simi wrote in her diary, 'but the spirits didn't want time to heal.' The spirit babies began smashing alarm clocks, watches, digital radio clocks, grandfather clocks and egg-timers onto the cracked

46

tarmac of the Harbour Road. The air was stung with the confused whir of seconds shattering. On their last evening together, Simi and the *abiku* man sat on the harbour wall and watched a P&O ferry rest on the skyline. The ship seemed immobile, and yet it had soon disappeared beyond the lighthouse, out of sight.

At this point, Simi's diary entries become sporadic. The pages are clogged with indecipherable scribbling that could be either words or pictures; it's impossible to tell. It seems Simi wallowed in her pain in the weeks that followed. Unable to tolerate his wife's mood swings, her naked wanderings and the way that she now screamed out another man's name in the middle of the night, her English husband moved out and filed for a divorce. Abeyomi reckons that, when the Englishman left, a couple of the spirit babies tagged along with him and pestered him for years to come.

'Simi soon became lonely in that house, surrounded by depressed spirits and unsold still lives,' my grandmother told me, 'so she moved back home with us.'

'Ach, sure, she'll get over it,' my grandfather Cathal suggested when the first wave of Simi's sadness flooded their house on Tivoli Avenue and killed off all the petunias. Abeyomi shook her head, wondering after forty years of marriage if this Irishman would ever learn. Surely everyone knows what happens when a spirit child sets their eye on something?

And initially Abeyomi presumed it was grief swelling inside Simi, making her belly bulge like a full moon. By the time Simi admitted that she was pregnant, she was already four and a half months. 'The child of a spirit child?' my grandmother almost choked when Simi told her the news.

Simi shrugged, 'Let's pray it's not bleedin' *abiku*, right?'

To my grandparents' surprise, in her third trimester Simi returned to her studio and began to paint again. In the

Encyclopaedia of Modern Art on my bookshelf, this period has become known as 'Simidele O'Doherty's Late Renaissance'. This is the phase by which art historians have been most fascinated. In one of the cut-outs I keep in my scrapbook, the renowned art critic Síle Reinhart wrote, 'It is no exaggeration to say the canvases produced by O'Doherty during this ninety-day period altered the course of Irish art history.'

On these stressed panels, spirits float along intricate Celtic spirals. I keep prints of my favourite pictures in my scrapbook. Sometimes I run my fingers along the colourful patterns, imagining how Simi splattered each canvas with paint until the pigments worked under her fingernails. In the only two surviving photos from this time, Simi resembles one of her own creations, with her wild hair, green eyes and paint-sparked skin.

Her diary describes how she painted each day until she was exhausted, and then threw herself down on the ground of her studio to sleep. 'There are no spirits with me these nights,' Simi wrote on her studio wall in spidery black paint. 'I left them all by the harbour wall with horizons draining from their eyes.' And one night, Simi did something she'd never done before, but had always known she was capable of. She read her own future and saw the desolation of life without her soulmate. She saw a single bed. Microwave dinners for one. Numbness, like being trapped in one of the low-lying clouds over Dublin. She saw that she would spend the rest of her life searching for a shard of emotion she would never feel again.

My grandmother often talks about how, when Simi's waters broke, the lights went out over half of Dublin Bay. Emergency generators kicked into motion, and the residents of the city were overwhelmed by a wave of nostalgia.

'Surely to God, she doesn't seem to want to live,' Doctor Casey in the Rotunda puzzled as she analysed the rain dance of Simi's slow green pulse. Sometimes the spirits would sneak inside Simi's heart monitor, causing it to tango with hope before the doctor's eyes. Other times the spirit babies would fart on the life-support machine, causing alarm bells to blare and stressing out the entire hospital.

As Abeyomi sat by her daughter's bedside, Simi's eyes were focussed on a landscape far away. 'I already knew she was gone,' my grandmother told me with tears in her mahogany eyes, 'and it was only then I realised the stupidity of placing human limits on an *abiku* child.' Until that moment, Abeyomi had failed to understand the truth about Simi. Her consciousness—her *Ori Orun*—could never be tied to human form. Simi did not fear death because her spirit was sure to continue, so what reason was there to feel frightened?

My mum was the great Irish artist Simidele O'Doherty. Family legend has it that just as Simi left this life I entered it, opening my earth-brown eyes with the wail of one whose spirit was entirely my own. They called me Ife, from the Yoruban word for love, and wrapped me in one of Simi's old blankets.

The rest of the story has been the subject of countless songs, books and biopics. No doubt you are familiar with the story of how the grief-stricken grandparents eventually brought themselves to clear out Simi's studio. Thinking to use the money towards my schooling, they started to auction off the paintings. Abeyomi and Cathal were shocked when their daughter's epic final works garnered seven-figure sums. 'We had no idea that her paintings would cause such a stir,' my grandmother told me.

I often wish my grandparents had kept the famous canvases, but over time I've come to settle for posters and the prints in my scrapbook. Many of Simi's masterpieces now grace the walls of embassies, government buildings and the drawing rooms of heads of state across the world. Her most famous painting, *Infinite Landscapes*, has pride of place in the National Gallery of Ireland, and I call in to see it on my way to work sometimes. Her legacy put me through college and secured my future. The *abiku* man never returned.

Meanwhile, as a baby I showed no signs of being a spirit child. I would doze in the cot where Abeyomi had left me, and would allow Cathal to cradle me for hours. My toddler years were marred by nothing more than spilt milk, crayoned-on wallpaper and the odd tantrum. But in the nights that followed, my grandparents always left my bedroom door ajar and a small pair of blunt-bladed scissors propped by my bedside with their legs wide open, just in case.

Ife O'Doherty, Dublin, 2015

Titanium Heart

The famous might of the Steel City had threaded through generations, dating back to when Sheffield was founded on the River Sheaf. City of knives. City of iron. Sheffield was forged in the furnaces of metal works dominating the skyline. It was a solid city. A grey city. A city that, it seemed, would never end. And yet Eva and Stephen were hardly surprised when they first noticed that Sheffield was melting.

In the Steel City, things started to disintegrate slowly. Eva would touch the steel bars of the empty cradle, only to find a thin film of silver coming away on her fingertips. Stephen would open a stainless-steel novel, only to discover the page numbers dripping out onto his lap and singeing his jeans. Eva woke up one Tuesday in their house on the top of the hill to find that the bedside lamp had melted into a silvery puddle, and later she stepped outside to find rows of galvanised starlings melted together on the telephone wires.

Neither of the lovers wanted to be the first to acknowledge that Sheffield was melting.

'Maybe we should leave, love,' Stephen suggested. 'There's nothing left for us here.'

'Everything's fine,' Eva retorted, as she sat in an opulent pearl-grey lake where their two-seater leather sofa used to be.

'But, babe …'.

'Just leave it, Stephen.' She turned away from him, and to Stephen it seemed like another lifetime in which he had first seen Eva dancing in the pulsing lights of The Leadmill Nightclub. She shivered and cupped a mug of coffee for warmth, although the house was melting around her.

The other citizens of Sheffield soon started to notice the melting issue too. One morning the people of Crookesmoor awoke to find that the number 52 buses were melting, their tyres oozing into the roads, over which a heat vapour shimmered. The helplines of the Sheffield City Bus Headquarters were hopping with calls from agitated passengers, all of which were completely pointless because the SCB Headquarters was melting and all the customer service operatives had long since left the building. In hillside estates, street lamps were softening and bending their necks like tired giraffes. Liquefied steel streamed down off the seven hills and into the valleys of Rivelin and Pitsmoor, where it cruised in playful rivulets, causing traffic chaos. Factories and museums were melting, and children were delighted when they had to be sent home from school because the schools were melting too.

The Steel City's citizens presumed, of course, that this was the evil and deliberate work of the Iron Master and his Metal Cabinet. When public anger eventually reached melting point, a delegation of residents marched off to the capital carrying indignant placards. *REAL* JUSTICE FOR *STEEL* CITY! SOLIDITY RULES! STOP SMELTING OUR CITY! Chaining themselves to the Iron Master's railings and throwing melted objects at his barred windows and using a blowtorch to melt down his letterbox was all to no avail: the Metal Cabinet simply closed their metal curtains and looked the other way. Tired and frustrated, the protesters returned to Sheffield several weeks later with their slogans buckled and their spirits tarnished and no solution reached.

Only Stephen suspected that the hairline fracture in Eva's titanium heart was somehow causing this meltdown. 'Give it up, love,' he coaxed her during another sleepless night in their house on the top of the hill. 'Just let it go.' But Eva simply stared at him with her steady grey eyes, and when she looked away Stephen felt as if all the sadness in the world had dug its claws inside him.

Grief and shock do strange things to a relationship, thought Eva, like molten lava silently oozing into crevices and changing the landscape.

Seasons passed. When it was sunny, reflected brightness off all the melting buildings caused an inferno of light, leaving several people blind. When it snowed, the spiralling flakes sizzled as they touched the scorching metal ground.

On the day Stephen left Sheffield, he parted from Eva at the Peace Garden steps, which had softened but hadn't melted yet. Eight looming chalices poured liquid ore into cascades at each entrance of the protractor-shaped gardens. Raindrops hissed and spat as they hit the hot street, and sulphuric steam rose up off the pavements. Humidity flushed the lovers' cheeks and dampened their hair, and Eva and Stephen looked like sticky red-faced newborns, distressed at the concept of living. 'It's for the best I go, love,' Stephen said, taking Eva's hand, surprised to find that her fingers were deep-river cold. 'We just can't go on like this.'

'I know,' she nodded, swallowing hard. She couldn't bring herself to look at Stephen's face, so she studied his knees instead; those worn-out jeans with the iron-ore stains on them. He had always found a practical solution to every conceivable problem, but had failed entirely to understand the acid guilt that was eating a slow hole inside her. In the space where Eva had cocooned their child for three months there was now just a black hole, which expanded every time Eva saw the new worry lines carved between Stephen's brows. If she'd been more careful, she thought, if she had rested more and taken the right vitamins, perhaps it wouldn't have happened. Perhaps they'd have a living baby instead of a slowly melting cot.

Unable to maintain a grip any longer, Eva let go of Stephen's hand. She turned and walked away from him into a bank of cloud, which sucked her silhouette until she dissolved completely. Stephen stood watching as the city flared up in a wild, insatiable crucible in Eva's wake.

Unseen and unmeasured, time kept turning. The courtin' couples at Coles Corner were startled from their embraces one frosty November night when a jagged volcanic gash split the street corner in two. Saturday shoppers on Fargate were stunned to see the cobbles of the pedestrianised street melt like lumps of jelly into a red-hot river. And the women on the backstreets of the Moor selling flowers stopped gossiping to listen to the eerie creaking made by the metallic fronts of the department stores as they sagged and folded into each other.

Alone in the house on the top of the hill, Eva waited patiently in the furnace of her thoughts and carefully dismantled herself into her elements. Night after night she picked up the past and stepped into the abyss of its melting mirror. Night after night she poured herself into a search for nuggets of reason, which she could never find. Until, one night, when all that was left of Eva was a pile of carbon, silicon and slack, the flames inside her ribcage finally began to dissipate. Shiny aluminium tears slid from Eva's grey eyes and trickled down her throat, and the shapeless cast that she had been cradling began to mould itself into the possibility of a life. And because the clock hands had warped so long ago, and the clock springs had distorted, no one in the Steel City could have told you whether it was one night or a thousand years later when Eva started to forgive herself.

Gradually, Sheffield stopped melting. The streets slowly solidified. And the councilors resourcefully employed themselves in dreaming up innovative ways to use all the melted-down metal. First they built a tram system of twenty-nine kilometres of cables and alloy tracks lassoed around the shoulders of the city, along which purple trams whizz cheerfully every ten minutes, apart from on Sundays and Bank Holidays. Next they commissioned an Olympic swimming pool with a monumental diving board and a stainless-steel water slide. New hotels sprang up along the crumbling canal banks, and the remainder of the metal was used to construct the bones of a gigantic shopping centre in a meadow on the eastern suburbs.

'Where's the Steel City?' thought Stephen, returning after many decades with the light gone out of his eyes, and finding himself lost in a city that was utterly unrecognisable. The cause of this, he quickly realised, was that the melted steel had been replaced by over two million trees. Sycamores yawned contentedly and stretched their arms into the sky. Fingers of ivy tickled the corners of ruined factory buildings. Silver birches posed around the Peace Garden steps, bathed in indigo up-lighting. Fairy lights winked and flirted amid the gently laughing leaves. In the newly built Tourist Information Office, an interactive touchscreen display informed Stephen that Sheffield now boasted more trees per capita than any other city in Europe. Indeed, the computer told him, the councilors were trying to change the city's nickname to Tree City, but this involved a lengthy bureaucratic process, you understand.

Nowadays only tepid cultural references to the Steel City remain. The refurbished Sheffield Railway Station with its impressive wrought-iron entrance. The flashy steel signage of the Crucible Theatre, and the trendy distressed-metal artwork in the Winter Gardens. And there, on the top of the highest of the seven hills, nestled in a grove of red-berried rowan trees, stands a steel statue of a beautiful, grey-eyed, sunlight-catching woman. Rusty leaves dance and shiver around the woman's shoulders, and in her arms she clutches a deathly small bundle, whose tiny fingers reach up towards her face. From the angle of the pedestal on which the woman stands, and the play of the phosphorescent light, Stephen could never work out in the end if she smiling, or weeping.

Under the Jasmine Tree

Virgin Maria del Carmen tells me in a dream that my son is coming. 'He'll arrive today' she whispers as she sprawls across a stall of tomatoes at the Mercado Alméda, her tarnished halo sending an eerie glow across the striped tarpaulin. Opening my eyes, I kiss my sleeping husband's shoulder. 'Maurizio! The boy is coming today!'

'Whatisit?' he rolls over. 'Hava email on your phone?'

'No, *cariño*, a dream.'

'*Madre de dios*,' he mumbles, his quick Sicilian accent slurred with tiredness, 'Jesús, Alma. Go back to sleep.'

For the next few hours I lie awake listening to the fading voices of Friday-night revellers below in Calle Siete Revueltas. With dawn the heat rises, and sun slants through our Venetian blinds, stapling the back wall with dashes of light. Slipping out of bed, I open our wardrobe to be greeted by an unfortunate jumble of garments. Pleated skirts. Frumpy jeans. Silk blouses with pinholes over the heart, left there by the needle of my badge from the Museo de Artes, *Alma – Receptionista* engraved in friendly cursive. A turquoise dress is the only splash of colour, and its hanger shrieks as I haul it from the wardrobe.

Downstairs in the kitchen I plunge the dress into a sink of soapy water, and the linen billows out. Turquoise tassels swirl like the searching fronds of a sea anemone. Wet dress dripping, I climb the spiral staircase to the white heat of the *azotea*, where I peg the dress to dry between red-brick chimney stacks.

It's August, and a feverish sense of expectation simmers in the streets of Seville. Along the River Guadalquivir, a group of young men are hanging lanterns for the Triana festival. One of them, perching on a rickety ladder, throws a bottle of water at the others, who dodge the spray, laughing. There's the tack, tack, tack of the young men's hammers, chains of lanterns rattling in their arms. Car windows flash and flicker along Avenída Cervantes. Even at this early hour, the heat of the roof terrace is unbearable, and it's a relief to return to the cool of the kitchen, where I turn on the espresso machine.

Maurizio is now singing 'My Way' in the courtyard, where he's polishing his good shoes for morning Mass. '*I did it myyy waaaaay*,' his voice echoes between sun-baked walls, a soft yet rough-edged baritone, not unlike the man himself, who now pads onto the flagstones of Casa Siete Revueltas. His bald head is already glistening with perspiration, his sleeves rolled up to reveal a lace of tattoos. He puts his polished shoes down on the kitchen table and scratches at the sacred heart on his elbow. 'Alma … you're not serious about this dream?'

'And why not?'

'Jesús, Alma.' He takes a crumpled handkerchief from his shirt pocket and sighs, as he does when I talk about miracles and cures and healing wells. He dabs the sweat from his temples. 'If anyone does turn up today … and they won't … he could be a lunatic. Some *ragazzo pazzo* looking for money.'

'Well, he can look all he likes.' My shrug indicates the ramshackle kitchen. The cracked mosaic above the worktop. The balky stove. The wonky table balanced on a tower of San Miguel coasters. Papery tentacles of spider plants reaching from overcrowded bookcases. Naked bulbs that flicker and buzz with dodgy electrics. Any trace of wealth has long since gone from the house my great-grandfather, the illustrious José Emmanuel Diaz, built in 1849 at the end of Calle Siete Revueltas, the most crooked street in Seville. A narrow series of bends and turns, each corner of the 'street of seven turnings' entices you to the next, so by the time you reach Casa Siete Revueltas you cannot remember where you came from or where you were heading.

'Still,' Maurizio persists, 'besides the dream.... This Irishman you've been in contact with, who the hell is he?'

'He's my son, Maurizio. We've been over this already. The agency said so.'

'And what about our girls? Alma, this is crazy.'

He's right, I suppose. My eldest, Isa, is studying social work in Madrid, calling me every other day to complain about the traffic, the heat, the Madrileños. The youngest, Sara, is spending her summer holiday at a surf camp in Cadiz, coming home sporadically with dreadlocked Catalan boyfriend in tow. Neither of them knows about this other child. Ciaran. The boy who would have been their elder half-brother. Ever since I saw that documentary, *Lost Spanish Babies*, on Telecinco last November, I've probably spent more time worrying about my son than either of my daughters. I watched the documentary on repeat and jotted down the number listed on the screen at the end of the credits. 'If you have been affected by any of the issues raised in tonight's programme …'.

Dialling the number in a trance, I didn't expect the sympathetic female voice at the end of the phone, or the

Search Reunion España forms, which arrived in the post within days.

Maurizio sighs, '*Va bene* … I'll leave you to it. At least you could let me stay, so you're not alone?'

'I'm not alone.' I tilt my chin towards the upper floors, where lime green *Lingua Fun Sevilla* T-shirts festoon the mahogany bannisters. The T-shirts, along with shoals of bright Havaianas flip-flops, have been left there by the American students renting our rooms for the summer. My dead mamma, who used to communicate with me regularly through angel readings and tarot cards, has gone on telepathic lockdown ever since we smashed up the interior of Casa Siete Revueltas three years ago. In the process, we converted the once high-ceilinged upper floors into compact study bedrooms, filling the stairwell with drumbeats, ringtones, shouts and squeals. The hallway rings with the clatter of feet as the students head out on Friday evenings, laughing and bumping into each other in short-sleeved shirts, sun dresses and heels. They reel home in the early hours, slam the heavy oak door and eat all the salami and mozzarella in the fridge. Now, Saturday morning, the silence of the upper floors is broken only by the tired, rhythmic creak of bedsprings. A pause. A young female voice. 'Baby, can you turn on the fan?'

Maurizio clears his throat. 'See you later.' He holds my shoulder for a second. 'Alma. For Christ's sake, call me if you need me, okay?'

I plant a kiss on his lips and he pulls back, jangles his keys and tucks his belly into his belt. I guess he's embarrassed, in the way that intimacy can be embarrassing between people as long married as we are. I wonder why Maurizio and I continue to communicate in English, although his Spanish is now fluent and my Italian passable. I suspect it's just a throwback to our courtship days, when English was our only common language. Perhaps our history is contained in the shapes of English. Or maybe it's just awkward to love someone in a language other than the one you started out in. Maurizio's newly polished size tens creak down the tiled hallway, and the front door clicks.

Climbing back up the stairs, I squint into the brightness of the roof terrace. Starched by the sun, my dress has dried in no time. A maxi-dress bought in a boutique in Granada some years ago, it's at least loose enough to disguise the jut of my ribs. Matching teal bangles jingle at my wrists as I fix my hair into a clasp and spray some Chance on my neck. When I return to the kitchen my mobile buzzes on the table. A missed call. A frantic voicemail. 'Mrs Diaz, this is Gabi from Search Reunion … just back from holiday … Ciaran requesting in-person meeting … one of the interns … gave your address by accident … protocol … urgent … call as soon as you …'.

Finding it hard to breathe, I take my iPad from my handbag and scroll through the morning's headlines. Pushing this aside, I take a notebook from a drawer. My pen hovers over a blank page, but as usual the words won't come. My upper lip twitches. Sweat gathers at the backs of my knees, the espresso machine hisses and the TV chatters as I sit in its blue glare and wait. *Dios te salve, Maria. Llena eres de gracia, El Señor es contigo….*

Around ten, the doorbell finally clangs, reverberating through the empty courtyard at the heart of Casa Siete Revueltas. As I hurry down the hallway, part of me longs to be proven wrong. To open the door and find our neighbour Antonella, or one of the American students. I can already taste the relief if this entire morning were to prove only a mix-up. I heave open the door and make a visor with my hand against blinding sunlight. *Ay dios mío.*

A lanky man in his early thirties stands on the doorstep, holding a small green cactus in a mosaic pot. He's wearing a pink linen shirt a size too big for him, but the devious Andalusian heat has made a mockery of his formality, and his collar is already ringed with sweat. He pushes his dark hair from his eyes. '*Tu ... es ... um ... estas ... Alma Diaz?*' he asks.

'Yes,' I answer.

'Oh, you speak English?' he says.

I try to smile, but my face feels as tight as a leather mask, and I know my smile must look slightly crazed.

'I am ...' he rubs the back of his head, 'at least I think I might be ...'.

'I know,' I tell him, and relief spreads across his face. 'You're Ciaran.'

'Right. Oh gosh, I was so worried. I spoke to a girl at the agency, but she wasn't sure if they'd be able to get hold of you on time. Did she speak to you?'

I nod, thinking that it's easier to lie than to explain that I was warned of his coming in a dream. Smiling now, the young man hands me the potted cactus. 'I'm so sorry I couldn't find you any flowers. I hope this is ... I hope it's okay.'

'It's beautiful.' I reach up to kiss his cheeks, and he fumbles, lunging one way and then the other, unfamiliar with the etiquette of Castilian kisses. '*Hijo.*' I breathe the word rather than say it as I hold my son for the first time in thirty-three years.

I take the cactus from him, and a memory blooms before me in the hot porch air. I remember lingering in the garden of Iglésia San Martín after Sunday Mass on a bright April afternoon in 1983, talking to the young deacon, Francisco. I was feeling confident in stonewashed jeans and a new denim jacket, my crimped hair stiff with cheap hairspray, my lips tacky with Pink Ice balm. We'd been talking for some time when Francisco placed a tight-lipped jasmine bud into my open palm. Holding my gaze, he closed my fingers around the flower and smiled as if we had settled something. I left the bud on my pillow that night to ward off mosquitoes and scare away evil spirits. Next morning, I awoke to an intoxicating perfume.

'Come in, come in.' I usher Ciaran down the shady hallway hung with portraits of dead relatives, and into the living room. A single ceiling fan is whirring like an asthmatic bumblebee struggling to take off, its yellowed slats barely managing to stir the morning heat. My son perches on the edge of one of the scratchy sofas, his eyes scanning the room, returning to the portrait of my dead mamma holding a stuffed parakeet. The air is heavy with the things we say and don't say. I ask him about his journey, and he compliments me on the house. Yes, the airport is convenient. Yes, the shuttle buses are very cheap. No, I haven't been to Ireland. Yes, it's an unusual house. Yes, it's true, my great-grandfather built it. We stick to the things we already know, retelling the basic details we have exchanged through Search Reunion España. He tells me that he's married, that he has a young daughter and that he's an architect and works for a small Dublin firm.

When he runs out of safe things to say, he clasps his hands nervously. 'It's a beautiful house. So strange to think of my grandparents, great-grandparents…. Sorry, Alma, I'm rambling here. My head is racing. I've been on holidays here in Seville the last week, but I just wasn't sure I'd pick up the courage. It was my wife who encouraged me to call on you. It's just so hard to know what to say.'

My dress is sticking to me. 'Perhaps we can walk? It would be easier?'

'That would be great.' He stands from the sofa, and a Bible topples off the slanted shelves of a nearby bookcase. He replaces it carefully. 'Sorry. Look at me, I'm wrecking the place.'

'Don't worry, there isn't much to wreck. Did you want to stay here with us? Your wife and daughter, will they come as well?'

'You're very kind, but I've to head home to Dublin tonight. Our flight's at ten. I left my wife and daughter by the pool, so they're happy out. My wife wanted to meet you too, but I felt … you know … I just needed to do this by myself.'

'I understand.'

As we step outside, heat rises from the cobblestones and from the greening manhole covers embossed with the city logo, '*No me ha dechado*', shortened to the symbol 'No8Do': Seville has not abandoned me. Leaving the twisting alleyway, we cross Plaza del Triumfo, through squares of shadow cast by terrace parasols. Our reflections glide across the window of Moda Nueva, where silver-faced mannequins pout in gaudy flamenco dresses.

Slowly, as if trying not to cause a wake in the liquid heat, we pass beneath the elegant lime trees of Plaza de la Encarnación, their smooth trunks dappled grey like beach pebbles. Finally I lead Ciaran down the steps at Metropol Parasol, and into Antiquarium Sevilla, a museum below street level that houses Seville's Roman and Moorish remains. Ciaran swivels to take in the expanse of the ruins. 'This is incredible. Imagine it all being preserved like this, right under the city's feet.'

Under dim blue lighting we follow a curving pathway through the antique ruins. Past kissing birds at the centre of a chipped mosaic floor. Fifth-century tiles depicting Medusa with her hair of writhing snakes. Columns and wells. Fish-salting vats. Arteries of forgotten streets, like deep lines carved in the city's wizened palm. We find a bench in front of one of the Roman settlements, and I slide the iPad from my handbag. 'I want to show you this.' My fingers swipe the screen.

GHOSTS OF FRANCO: LOST SPANISH BABIES
Charges are currently being investigated that thousands of Spanish infants were illegally abducted and sold for adoption over a forty-year period, until as late as the 1980s. What is believed to have begun as a political retaliation against leftist families during the dictatorship of General Francisco Franco evolved into a global trafficking business involving doctors, nurses and even nuns who colluded to....

The nun's habit was impossibly white. I watched her fingers as she was explaining my baby's death. Those pallid fingers gripped and twisted each other, like clown fingers trying to perform a circus trick. Then she placed a frozen child into my arms and stood back to see my reaction. From above the barred window of my hospital room, Virgin Maria was watching too with chipped blue eyes. The baby was heavy, and I cried because its lips were purplish and its chubby fingers were unresponsive to my touch. I cried, but I knew it was not my baby.

'Are you all right?' Ciaran says. 'You've gone very pale.'

'I think I need some air.'

We leave the ruins and take the elevator to the café on the terrace of Metropol Parasol. It's baking up here, and you can see the glistening mirage of Seville, with the glassy-green river snaking past the prison of Torre del Oro. My son looks down at me with concern, and I catch again the resemblance to Francisco, who was solemn in his white robes and heavy-rimmed glasses, holding the Bible for Padre Marquez and frowning intently. Mamma leaned across me to whisper to Tia Agnes, 'That's the new deacon. He's from Galicia.'

Francisco looked different, and when Padre Marquez introduced us to him at the end of Mass, he spoke differently too. He didn't have the Sevillian lisp that I'd grown up with, where words tumble into each other without edges or corners. Each of Francisco's words was distinct; his voice rocked with the rhythms of the sea. Behind his glasses, his eyes met mine with total honesty, and for a moment we just looked at each other. When our gaze was broken, the world had changed.

There were words of course. Our conversations would stretch across days, weeks. We would often tease each other in the sacristy, where I helped Mamma and the other sacristans to clean the candleholders, patch the kneelers or fix the binding on hymn books. I remember listening to Francisco's lilting Galician stories while I polished my many gilded reflections on the chalice. There was a story about a sea kelpie, and another about a Galician fishing boat that drifted and was rescued close to the Arctic Circle. But his words were the first thing to evaporate from my mind. Apart from a few sentences and exclamations, all I have is images revisited so often they've become smooth as sea-worn stones. They say each time we revisit a memory, we change it.

Ciaran leads me to a table at the corner of the terrace and pulls out a red plastic chair. 'I'm so sorry. This must be a shock, me turning up like this. I don't know what I was thinking of. In my head, I thought it would be easier.'

'It's okay.' I try to smile. 'I knew you were coming.'

We order two cold glasses of San Miguel, and I study my son's narrow face. His sallow skin has been deprived of sunlight for so long it has drained to the colour of old books. He's mine, and yet not mine. Nothing should surprise me about this stranger, and yet I'm taken aback when he takes out a pack of Lucky Strikes and lights one up. 'You live in Ireland?'

'Yes,' he smiles. 'By the way, I read *Under the Jasmine Tree*. Your poems are wonderful.'

'That was ten years ago,' I laugh. 'I'm surprised you found a copy.'

There passes an angel; that's what we *Sevillanos* say when there is a sudden silence between two people like this. *Bendita tú eres entre todas las mujeres. Y bendito es el fruto de tu vientre: Jesús.* My son shifts in his chair and stubs the butt of his cigarette into one of the white ceramic ashtrays. 'It's so hard to know where to start. Forgive me for asking, but you must have been very young when … when …'.

'Sixteen,' I reply. My sixteenth birthday fell on the feast of Virgin Maria del Carmen, and at the parade I stood in the heat of the assembled crowd, where the drumbeat steadily quickened. Brass instruments and gold buttons gleamed.

My skin was coated in a film of sweat, strands of hair stuck to my forehead, and I could feel the bulge of my breasts in the girlish dress Mamma had made me wear. Ahead of me, Mamma fussed over the altar boys, straightening their robes and spitting on her palm to pat down their hair. She didn't look back. And all the people were watching me watching Francisco. Then everything was far away and I was watching it from under water, where the sound couldn't reach.

'Alma, Alma!' I woke surrounded by people's dusty ankles. 'Alma,' Francisco's breath tickled my cheek, 'come, come, you've fainted, Alma. Let's get you some water.'

Alone with Francisco in the sacristy, I felt the weight of what was about to happen shiver between us. The mahogany wood of the tabernacle gleamed. The rush of sound from the procession outside sounded like the throb of a nearby ocean. Francisco hurried over and put a damp cloth to my forehead. I placed my hand over his.

And on the terrace table, thirty-three years sit between me and my son. He smiles at me, and when he takes off his sunglasses I'm surprised to see tears at the corners of his eyes. He wipes them with a napkin, blows his nose and laughs. 'Sorry. Embarrassing myself. It's just so strange, finally meeting like this.'

I take his hand.

Later, when I'm paying the waiter, Ciaran opens his wallet and takes out a five euro note, which he tucks under the ashtray. In the plastic pouch at the front of his wallet, a photo catches my eye. In its well-worn creases I see my son held in the embrace of an older couple. 'Is that your parents?'

'That's right.' He wriggles the picture out of its pouch and hands it to me.

'They look lovely.'

'They're great, they really are. Brilliant parents, brilliant grandparents, but it's just been difficult with them lately. I just wish they'd told me. I always knew I was adopted … but I always thought I was Irish. It wasn't until I started doing my own research that I found out … that I found out about you.' He shakes his head at the ground, and I know the question he's going to ask. 'And my father, Alma, if you don't mind me asking, was he from Seville too?'

I mess with a coaster, avoiding his eyes. 'We couldn't be together. That's why they took you. I don't remember his name.' I can see the nebulas of further questions clouding Ciaran's eyes, but I touch his hand. 'Maybe we'll go now?'

Leaving the café, our shadows merge as we fall into step with each other. Seeing the city through Ciaran's eyes, it strikes me that nothing is as it seems in Seville. Moorish arches vie with crucifixes in a city scarred by conquests, each building morphed out of what went before. We stroll the spiked palm shade of the Alcazar Gardens, lunch at a tiny tapas bar in Triana, and visit Universidad de Sevilla, housed in a former cigarette factory. Ciaran whistles at Arabic courtyards, marble fountains and carvings of galleons around the grand university entrance. 'Do you happen to know how old this is?' he asks.

I have no exact answers for him, and the topics of conversation swing from Irish weather to Spanish history, at which point I feel as if I'm reciting one of the tourist information booklets from my work.

Who is this man, this blood of my blood? He is now just a few years older than Christ when he surfaced from his lost years; from the child found teaching in the temple, to the man who stepped into the Jordan to be baptised by John. How can I begin to understand Ciaran, who he is, where he's been? In the thirty-three years since he was taken, he has become Irish. All I've ever seen of his country is the vivid green landscape Irene sent to me on a postcard once. In that picture, inquisitive-looking sheep were blocking a road that wormed into rough blue hills underneath which the caption read *Rush Hour, Donegal.*

I had developed a story of my son, an image of how he would be. I've been waiting for him for thirty-three years, and now he's walking next to me, I am waiting still.

We return home through streets that judder with the sound of shutters being slammed closed for siesta. Canopies of white tarpaulin have been stretched between the rooftops of Calle Imagen and Calle Alcázares, and the pavements undulate with warm blue shadows, across which our sandals lisp.

'Will you stay for dinner?' I ask when we return to Casa Siete Revueltas.

'I really should go soon,' Ciaran says, 'but it would be lovely to stay with you a while. I'll just step out for a second to ring my wife and let her know how we're getting on. She'll be worrying.'

'Take your time.'

'Thanks.' Forgetting about the Castilian kisses, he wraps me in a hug that smells of sunlight and cigarettes.

Francisco's robes smelt of incense, and afterwards my skin smelt of incense too. I washed it away in the shower that night; the incense smell along with the thin blood that trickled down between my thighs. 'No one will come in,' Francisco whispered to me, '*cariña* ... no one will know.' But I saw the black eyes of Virgin Maria del Carmen watching me over his shoulder.

The sounds of Seville have followed me into Casa Siete Revueltas tonight. As I go about making dinner, crushing garlic and peeling onions, I imagine the walls of this old house are porous, like a coral reef, absorbing each shift in the city's mood. Each lull. Each spite. Each fever. Over the river the Triana festival has begun, and the night is full of the melancholy of flamenco guitar.

I first felt my son's physical presence during Mass, when we stood for the gospel. There was a tight sensation in my belly whenever I stood up or stretched. My breasts swelled and I felt as clumsy-footed as a calf. Initially it was only whispers behind clicking fans at the Mercado Inglés. '*The daughter of Emmanuel Diaz Perez ... must be turning in his grave ... after his death, still living in that grotesque mansion ... that horrible, dark, twisted street ... see what happens when a girl is raised without a father?*' Mamma ignored these rumours, her head held high beneath her black mantilla. But then she locked the heavy door of Casa Siete Revueltas and banned me from leaving the house.

One day, at about seven months, I crept out. The smell of blood was in the streets. A crowd was dispersing from the Plaza del Torres, leaving the corpse of the bull behind. From across the street, the statue of Carmen looked on, desolate. After pushing though the crowds for an hour, I turned homewards. I had nowhere else to go. My son came to me on a September day when the heat had matured into sultry warmth and the leaves along the Guadalquivir were starting to wither like old paper. I held Ciaran only once before they took him away.

'Well?' Maurizio enters the kitchen, where I'm skinning chorizo and dicing it into chunks. I hand him Ciaran's photo and he takes out his reading glasses.

Against a backdrop of autumn leaves, Ciaran is laughing into the camera as if he's just shared a joke with his parents. It reminds me of Isa's graduation and that bright October sky framed by the quadrangle of Salamanca University. Maurizio proudly filming the event on his new video camera, which, we later discovered, he had put on the wrong setting, so all that can be seen of Isa's ceremony is the blurry shapes of things that may or may not have happened. 'Hmph,' Maurizio snorts, 'he doesn't look Spanish.'

I snatch the photo back and smooth the creases against my pinstriped apron. 'How would you know? You're not Spanish either.'

Hurt darts across my husband's brow. I want to take my words back, but there's no way to unsay them. He takes off his glasses and folds them back into his leather case. I catch a glimpse of the post-it note carefully taped inside the lid. *Isa (hija): 098 876 2637. Sara (otra hija): 099 178 3748. ESPOSA: 098 187 2736.*

Red mess now splutters in the cooking pot, a mixture of canned tomatoes from Lidl, kidney beans, leftover mince and scraps of chorizo. I stir the unappetising concoction, which I'll attempt to pass off to the Americans as 'local cuisine'. The first of the students now trudges into the kitchen, her blonde hair trailing down her back in a seaweed-like clump, Lingua Fun T-shirt mapped with sweat. 'Good day in class?' I ask.

'Man, those Spanish kids are horrible.' She takes a seat at one of the tables and hunches over her mobile.

Ciaran ducks into the kitchen apologetically. 'It smells delicious in here.'

'Spanish stew.'

'This looks amazing.' He hugs my shoulder. 'If only I had inherited your cooking skills, Alma.'

Maurizio picks up his keys. 'I'm off to adoration.'

How easily I retreat into myself. Looking at my husband now, it's as if he's just landed from another continent, or time-travelled to me across several decades. He looks as if he's about to say something, but then he glances at Ciaran and changes his mind.

As Maurizio walks out, I turn back to Ciaran. 'Do you have to go soon?'

'Unfortunately,' he replies. 'I'm kicking myself for leaving all this to the last minute. I wish we'd had longer. We'll keep in touch though, won't we, Alma?'

'Of course.'

He smiles down at me and my feeling of tenderness towards him tilts into the unbearable. In this moment I have the acute sensation that I am splitting in two. No matter how hard I try to keep my skin together, my organs are dividing and pieces of me are spilling all over the dark-veined tiles of Casa Siete Revueltas. A voice lifts from within me. 'Just one minute.' I step out of the kitchen and down the gloomy hallway, under the disapproving glares of all my dead relatives. I don't start to run until I have pushed open the front door and stepped out into the darkness of the street.

Laughter now ricochets from bars at the edges of Plaza Concepcion. Horses stamp in their hot shadows around the cathedral. A car backfires somewhere over the river, and a gypsy girl wanders between terraces, cradling a bucket of plastic roses. A group of Japanese tourists follow a guide with a white umbrella, who points out, 'Here is the barrio where the port once stood. All this was under water.' Down the side street of Calle Imagen, a tiny chaplet blazes lantern-bright between closed shutters. The chapel is the size of a telephone kiosk, and can only hold only an altar, an adorer and a candlelit statue of the Madonna. I push open the glass door and drop to my knees, breathing in the mustiness of incense.

Below the tabernacle, Virgen Maria del Carmen poses in supplication. '*Jesus, Alma,*' her heavenward eyes seem to say, '*Look at the mess you have yourself in.*' Kneeling under the baroque altar with its elaborate carvings of saints, martyrs and overfed cherubs, I have the feeling the chapel is about to collapse on me. In a type of reverse vertigo, I imagine being crushed under the weight of solid gold. *Santa María, Madre de Dios, ruega por nosotros pecadores, ahora y en la hora de nuestra muerte.*

There are things Ciaran will never know, and things I cannot tell him. Like how I stood apart from the others on the night of Francisco's ordination, waiting in the silence under the jasmine tree. How the leaves were a dark mesh creeping over the church wall, and how the fading white blossoms parted their skirts to send the last of their heady sweetness into the still night air. I could never tell Ciaran how, after I'd waited a long time, Francisco came to me. 'Alma,' he said. His voice was as rough as sea spray, as if he were being choked by the clerical collar that now ringed his neck. Silently I plucked a wilting jasmine flower from a branch above my head and placed it into Francisco's palm.

It's dark when I step out of the chaplet, back into the humid caress of the night heat. I retrace my steps along Calle Almésa, and I stop at the corner of Plaza del Triumfo, close to the Archivo del Indies. Within a few minutes, Ciaran emerges from the mouth of Calle Siete Revueltas, and from here I watch him walking slowly with his head down and his hands in his pockets. Waiters beckon to him, trying to entice him with their colourful menus, but he shakes his head. Conversations continue, oblivious to his passing. Glasses clink, guitar music drifts, and the girl selling roses is shooed away from one of the bars. Something is eating the palms in Seville. Close to where I'm hiding, the palm trunk has been gnawed into a honeycomb of holes and is cordoned off in case the tree falls.

I know Ciaran will never return down the winding street to Casa Siete Revueltas. Perhaps he'll email me eventually, but he'll be relieved when I don't reply, and the memory of sunlight moving across the café table at Metropol Parasol will become buried in other memories of things that didn't quite work out. It's only now I realise the meaning of the dream sent by Virgin Maria del Carmen. It did not herald my son's arrival, but his departure. My letting go.

As Ciaran nears the middle of the plaza, a three-year-old girl runs and grabs him around the knees. She's followed by a woman with curly hair tied in a loose bun, wearing shorts and a flowing kaftan, who rolls a suitcase to a halt on the cobbles and touches his arm in concern. From Ciaran's helpless hand gestures I can imagine what he's saying. 'The day went fine, we seemed to be getting on really well ... but then she just disappeared. I don't know what I did wrong.' The woman rubs his arm and hugs him tightly, and the little girl tugs her sleeve and shouts, 'Mammy, Mammy, Mammy!'

Arms linked, the family disappears across the plaza, into the leisurely mingle of well-dressed people out for the evening *paseo*. Church bells chime for evening Mass at the cathedral, and I remember turning away from Francisco on that last day in the gardens of Iglésia San Martín. Crimped hair, a denim jacket and stonewashed jeans that fitted again after the stretch of nine months. Seventeen years old and determined not to cry, I walked away from Francisco and out of the gardens. Keeping to the shadows, I turned back up the hot street, into a heat-haze that blurred and distorted the distance.

On Cosmology

A three-week-old foetus, according to Google Images, is a gooey alien-like creature, soft as an oyster. If that in any way resembles you, could you please give me a sign or something? I know it's too early for you to kick, unless you are a super-advanced space-age zygote. But if you could just give me some symptoms then I'd know for sure. Despite having made a career in science, I never was much good at biology. 'Zygote' is a new word for me. I only learnt it yesterday when I googled 'three weeks pregnant'.

The early December air is festering with decaying leaves, the colours of a smashed-up sunset. A late autumn this year, they said on Newstalk when I was driving to work this morning, because of the record-breaking heat this summer, which has caused abnormally high sugar levels in the leaves. The Christmas tree in Trinity's front square has blown over and lies in a sparkling heap. I feel like Christmas is happening in another solar system from where I am. For three weeks, all I've thought about is you.

I suppose, little zygote, you're wondering how you got here. Well, that makes two of us. Your father said our encounter was 'passionate'. But I can tell you now, there was nothing 'passionate' about the bruise the colour of cheese mould that he left on the inside of my thigh. If you *do* exist, I guess you'll want to know about your father. David is a six-foot-something game designer from New York with natty brown dreadlocks and a deep voice. His shoes are spaceships. Even his hazel eyes are massive, magnified by black-rimmed glasses.

We met a month ago at the opening of Cosmos, an astrophotography exhibition at the Dublin Science Gallery. Sipping free Aldi chardonnay in the echoing glass-walled lobby, we lingered before a wall-to-floor image of a single hawthorn tree silhouetted against a mess of stars. We'd been talking for a while when David turned to me. 'Sinéad, tell me, what do you lecture in?'

'Just first year stuff mostly,' I replied. 'And the Periastron.'

David nodded. 'We should go out sometime.'

I'd had a glass and a half of the tangy yellow wine, and I was wearing a new jumper-dress that made me feel more confident than usual, so I said yes.

Two nights later, a Tuesday as I remember it, we sipped cokes and small-talked in the Gourmet Burger Kitchen before going to see a French film about a blind contortionist who is trying to find his long-lost lover in the streets of Léon. David kissed me passionately in the back row. 'God, you're sexy,' he whispered.

As first dates go, it had been pleasant enough. But when I arrived home to my attic apartment in Phibsborough, I pulled off my purple snood to find an ugly bruise on my neck the colour of summer fruit about to darken into sticky-sweet rot. I googled 'how to get rid of a hickey fast', and Google advised me to apply an ice compress and to brush the area with a toothbrush to regain circulation. So I found myself at 2:05 a.m. with a bag of frozen veg pressed against the soft flesh under my jaw, an electric toothbrush in my hand. If you'd seen me, you'd have laughed.

The hickey was all the more mortifying because I was meeting my mum the next day, and she's the type of Irish mammy who can smell a love bite before it even happens. Even worse, one of the undergrads in my Wednesday-morning tutorial on 'The Importance of Tides for Periastron Precision' spotted the hickey straight off when I was chalking the formula $\Delta\Theta_p = ((\pi c^2 \Lambda a^3)/GM)\sqrt{(1-e^2)}$ onto the blackboard. My student, a greasy lad from Kuwait, cast me a toxic look that might have been test-tubed and labelled *Dark Disdain*. After lunch I looped my snood round my neck strategically and drove to Heuston to meet my mum off the Sligo train. And even though she didn't notice the hickey, I still felt like crap.

Our second date should never have happened. After the love bite I had sworn I was never going to see your father again. But I longed for the closeness of him. So, like an eejit, I waited at the Spire one November night, shivering in a black miniskirt, ankle boots and purple tights. And as I stood in the roaring neon rush of O'Connell Street, I rehearsed the reasons why I shouldn't sleep with David. There were plenty of reasons. He was clearly a player, and would finish with me as soon as we'd had sex. At the age of thirty I had turned a corner and was now making Positive Life Decisions. Plus, he was the type of guy who was used to getting everything he wanted, and I wasn't about to give him the satisfaction. But my breasts were traitors, shouting to be caressed. My skin was singing to be touched. The evening had a thunderstorm inevitability about it. And when we ended up naked in my bed, I don't think either of us was surprised.

'Did that feel good?' David asked, pulling away a short while later.

'Yeah,' I lied.

Then I noticed the shrivelled snake-skin of the condom by my nightstand. 'Hang on ... did you just...?'

'Yeah.' He grinned goofily, as if he'd been caught stealing cookies or spilling milk on the best tablecloth.

'But I'm not on the ... and you're not wearing the ...'.

'Oh.' He searched the ceiling as if the right words were hidden there. 'Well there are pills for that, right? I mean, don't worry.'

Well, little zygote, my eyes welled up. I don't know if it was tiredness, or the fact that David hadn't even asked permission before emptying himself into me. I hid behind my hair and tried to wipe my eyes discreetly. 'Hey,' David said, 'what's wrong? Are you crying?'

'No ... no, I'm not. I guess I'm coming down with a cold or something.' I slid from the bed, grabbed the twisted figure-eight of my black knickers from the sand-coloured carpet, and stumbled into the en-suite bathroom. I blew my nose on some toilet roll and rubbed the gritty mascara smudges from under my eyes.

Desolate is not a word we get to use very often. We lay under my blue, lily-patterned duvet with the TV on mute, and I stayed awake, staring at the screen long after David had started snoring. On Christmas ads, families smiled so much I thought their faces might break, shooting white-polished teeth into each other's cheeks. Glossy-haired couples held hands and frolicked in fake machine-snow.

Next morning, I awoke to the rattle of rain on the skylight, my fingers reeking of latex and sour sweat. I lifted the cheerful turquoise corner of a Durex wrapper from beside my bed and dropped it into the bin. As I did so,

I considered that this particular condom had failed in its mission in life. David had only worn it for less than two seconds before whipping it off just in time to impregnate me. We fumbled around for our clothes in the red-stained dark. I guess I could have turned on the light, or pulled the blinds, but that didn't occur to me at the time. Or perhaps the blood-red shadows just suited my mood.

Wipers swished the silence back and forth between us as I drove into the city. Obviously feeling the awkwardness, David began telling me about the latest game he was designing. 'It's a quest narrative,' he said. 'You remember those teenage novels where the reader gets to decide the plot? If you want x to happen, go to page y … it's a bit like that. The storyboarding for it is insane. You have to think of so many different threads.' Pulling into a cycle lane, I dropped him off at a bus stop on my way to Trinity. 'Don't forget to go to the pharmacy' were his last words to me before he stooped out of the car.

I didn't bother replying.

After mumbling through my first lecture on 'Calculating the Periastron Using Infrared', I pulled on my leather jacket and hurried up Grafton Street, slicing a pathway through the crowds with my starry umbrella.

Boots pharmacy smelt of wet feet and spilt mouthwash. 'Can I speak to a pharmacist?' I asked the sales assistant.

'Sure,' he smiled, 'just wait here.'

I lingered next to the display of pre-conception lubricants, in front of the stand of Rapid Fix Nail Varnish. Then a squirrelly haired pharmacist beckoned me to a consultation cubicle at the side of the counter. He nodded while I explained my predicament, before asking, 'Did it happen within the last twenty-four hours?'

'Yes,' I said, cringing at the loaded implication of the word 'it'. The pharmacist's face was so kind I wanted to hug him and put spidery mascara stains all over his crisp blue shirt. After taking my blood pressure he gave me a white tablet packaged in a sheet of orange foil. 'Make sure you take this with food,' he said. Then he handed me a pink Emergency Contraception leaflet with an empty speech-bubble on the cover.

On my way to the till, I picked up a bottle of Lucozade and one of those Rapid Fix Nail Varnishes in a shade called Flawless Nude. I paid by card and hurried back to Trinity, through seeping rain that clung to my hair in a fine mist.

Awkward with my bulging handbag and dripping umbrella, I locked myself in one of the arts block's toilets, dimly lit by vein-concealing blue blubs. On the cubicle door a poster girl daydreamed under the heading *Have You Got Thrush?* Generations of students had markered the plastic walls with logos. *i live in hope, i sleep in rathmines. Ben + Jess did it here 19/3/2012. I just wrote on a wall, take THAT society. Shit happens :)*

As I perched on the toilet lid with the pill on my index finger, the thought ducked across my mind: *I could keep David's child.* I studied the tablet, trying not to listen to the pissing from other cubicles. I could steal the child inside me and raise it as a single mum. Then I wouldn't be alone any more. At least with you around I'd have a bit of company. *Stupid idea.* I threw the thought away and swallowed the pill with a fizzy gulp of Lucozade. I don't know why I expected that small white tablet to turn back time and dissolve my worries.

And now it's been three weeks. Technically, little zygote, you shouldn't exist, because the morning-after pill has a 95 per cent success rate. But 5 per cent is still plenty of kids, and I have a feeling you might be one of them.

I've been living on packet soup for three weeks. The milk in my fridge is gradually changing itself into cottage cheese, while the lemons on my shelf are doing a fairly successful job of metamorphosing into powdery blue penicillin. I observe these changes as if through the wrong end of a telescope. When I'm not lecturing on the Periastron, or sitting in the Berkeley Library staring across the frozen cricket lawn, I spend most of my time at home on my laptop googling 'early signs of pregnancy'. But this is a farcical exercise; every time I read about a symptom it immediately manifests itself in me. *Increased saliva*: my mouth waters. *Abdominal pain*: my belly aches. *Swollen breasts*: I unhook my bra to study the reflection of my breasts from multiple angles in the bathroom mirror before concluding I have no idea what size or shape they were to start off with.

One night, close to 4:00 a.m., after three cups of black coffee and half a bottle of pinot grigio, I opened my laptop and googled 'abortion clinics UK'. Friendly websites with discreet fonts rushed to my aid immediately, but when I clicked on one of them my throat tightened. I closed the tab, deleted my internet history and started a different search. This time I saw a ball of cells multiplying with fierce determination, amniotic fluid gathering to cushion their swell. I saw oxygen gushing through microscopic channels. I closed the laptop gently. It's still too early for me to do a pregnancy test. For now, all I can do is wait.

You know, just the other day I had a text from your father. *Hey there Sinéad, how are you? Maybe we could get together sometime?*

What is this guy's problem? Wasn't our last encounter bad enough? Is he looking for a sequel? I'm baffled by the possibility that other people may have had even worse experiences of love than me. That we are all just floating around, colliding with each other like asteroids before being thrown even farther apart. That even at our most intimate, the distance between people is wide as the Periastron, the closest meeting point between any two stars.

Driving home today after my lecture on 'Detectability of Exoplanet Periastron Passage in the Infrared', I realised I'd had enough. I couldn't face going home to my empty flat, where I'd just be thinking about you, googling and trying not to text your father. So, I took a left onto George's Street and kept driving, onto the Rathmines Road, through the suburbs of Rathgar and Rathfarnham and out of the city. I kept on going until I was in the Wicklow Mountains, and I followed the brown-and-white tourist signs to Glendalough.

It was bleak out there. I mean, *bleak*. I parked at the upper lake, where a pack of gaudy-coated Italian teenagers slouched miserably around a coffee dock as if queuing for the apocalypse. Squelching through puddles, I followed the half-submerged pathway past the rippled tinfoil of the lake, across which a belligerent wind was howling. As I walked, the rain lifted a little and everything got very still under the mossy green pines. I'm not much of a climber. It must be over a decade since I really climbed anywhere. But on a mad impulse I started up these wooden planks, nailed into long steps leading through dense forest, up the mountainside.

I struggled up the steep incline, overtaken by several *actual* climbers wearing *actual* climbing gear. 'Grand day,' they called out to me without slowing down. Halfway up, I thought I might die. Sweat steamed off me, and I stripped off my jumper and leather jacket, down to my vest top. A creepy mist was coming down off the pines, and eerie bird calls sounded from within the drizzle, but I kept climbing until I had a chink of sky to aim for.

Gasping, I struggled out of the treeline. And you'd want to see the view from up there, little zygote. Purple-mapped mountains in all directions. The lake, curved like a silver willow leaf. And I just stood there, breath catching like brine in my throat, heart jabbing my chest, looking down the valley towards where Dublin cowered in the dip of hills. And your father, and Trinity, and the pharmacy where maybe next week I'll buy a pregnancy test.

A Baltic wind whistled over my bare shoulders, and I remembered when my sisters and I used to swim in the Atlantic as kids. When we'd had enough of the icy water, we'd slipslap out of the waves and run up the beach, skins tinged a deathly hue. And Mam wouldn't towel-dry us straight away, but would let us shiver for a few minutes because she'd heard on RTÉ that the shock of the towel-heat might kill us. Now I stood, trembling and burning and feeling my heartbeat steadying. Knowing I would have to head back down the mountain soon. Hoping I would make it through the forest before dark.

How to Learn Irish in Seventeen Steps

Step 1: Receive a letter with a fish jumping through a turquoise box in one corner. Unfold heavy blue-lined paper, translate neat black font into Portuguese and laugh. *Condicional?* They have got to be kidding. *A Chara*, Ms Luana Paula de Silva, thank you for registering with the Irish Teaching Council. Your registration is: CONDITIONAL. Your conditions are as follows: Irish Language Requirement. Time allowed: THREE YEARS.

During the first two years, you should:

Give in and bring Séan to Caraguatatuba, deep in the green belt of the Mata Atlântica, where Speak-Easy English School is seeking two new teachers. Over the next eighteen months, Séan's pale cheeks will freckle into a blotchy tan, fine lines will branch around his pond-green eyes, and he'll wear his thinning brown hair in a sweaty ponytail against the heat. Sometimes, on chirruping cricket-loud nights, Séan will play his guitar to you down on the *praia*, where skeletons of tiny crabs litter the damp white sand.

Celebrate your twenty-eighth birthday with runny chocolate pizza, Brahma beer and shots of cachaça. Try to teach Séan some Portuguese (he will never progress beyond *obrigada* and *cerveja por favor*).

Spilt the seam of your white chiffon dress thirteen minutes before you walk up the aisle in São Paulo. Your mama will stitch you back together, and her darting needle will prick your nutmeg skin. At this moment, your honey-brown hair should be sculpted into coils, and your mama's hands will be like frantic sparrows fluttering around your waist. Close your eyes and kiss the tarnished silver amulet of the *sorte* necklace your papa gave you.

Pose for photos with your new Irish in-laws against a sky of postcard blue. Hand-feed Séan *coxinha* and *pão de queijo*. Laugh when he takes pictures of the oozing *misto-quente* and black-bean *feijoada*.

Wrap your thighs around your new husband in the bathroom of the flat where you grew up, the back of your head rubbing against the yellowing fleur-de-lis wallpaper. Float hand-in-hand through the rippling palm shade of Moema and along Avenida Paulista, lined by its collar of skyscrapers. Take selfies in Parque Iberapuera in front of the towering banyan trees, their hanging roots like dark brown dreadlocks.

Hug your mama in the glass-walled departures lounge at Guarulhos Airport and feel as if you have stepped outside your body. Whisper, 'I'll be home soon,' into your mama's crimped black hair and inhale her lavender musk. Your head should be crowded with voices begging you to stay.

Don't sleep during the sixteen-hour flight back to Europe. While Séan snores with his head on your shoulder, stare out at the pulsing ice-blue lights on the wing. Imagine the path you are charting through the mess of Atlantic stars, which will make you feel lost in the snow globe of space.

Step 2: Watch swallows perform roller-coaster dips and dives across the pale June sky. You now have less than ten months in which to learn Irish. Post a cheque for two thousand euro to register for the *Scrúdú le hAghaidh Cáilíochta sa Ghaeilge.* Séan will ruffle your hair and say: 'Seriously, babe? You think you can learn Irish in ten months? That's insane!' Fold your arms. Think: how hard can this language be?

Click 'send' on your two hundred and fifty-sixth teaching application. Start each cover email 'Dear Sir/ Madam, I am a fully qualified primary school teacher with five years' teaching experience.' Drive the dank maze of Dublin streets in your silver Micra, delivering your neatly folded CV into the hands of various school secretaries, none of whom will ever contact you. After you have driven in the wrong direction up a bus lane for the third time in a week, Séan will buy you a satnav. Path-Finder98: Find Your Way Always. He will kiss your forehead. 'No more getting lost, babe, yeah?'

Dye your hair Caramel Blonde. Put on five pounds. Haul your end of the leather sofa sideways through the narrow hallway of a red-bricked terrace with a purple door. Tentacles of ivy should crawl over your pebble-dashed walls from Glasnevin Cemetery. To fill the blank page of another jobless day, take a walk from your new house to the graveyard. Circle-headed Celtic crosses will resemble rows of people watching an invisible opera. Black yew berries will bleed onto the gravel path, and the industrial growl of a lawnmower will drown out the silence. Try to whisper the Gaelic inscriptions to yourself and wonder what they mean. *Go dtaga do Ríocht. Go ndéantar do thoil. I bParthas na ngrást go rabhaimid.* The chop of a spade will startle you from your contemplation. Your stomach muscles will tauten at the sight of a gravedigger slicing into the daisy-strewn lawn. Kiss your *sorte* necklace and try not to remember the undertaker's black-gloved hands at your papa's funeral.

Love the way your husband wears his long hair in a batik bandanna and strides around your new home like Kurt Cobain storming across stage. Watch him drilling holes in the freshly painted magenta walls, polishing his Vespa in the driveway and perching on stacks of cardboard boxes in the sitting room, practising his guitar. Drag Gabriela to every gig performed by Séan's band, Rootless Drifters. Feel blessed to be privy to the secret vulnerabilities of this confident man, his bottle of anti-hair-loss shampoo packaged like a petrol can, and the greenish skull tattoo on his left bicep, which he regrets. Happiness will swell in your belly, leaving you freefalling in a sense of joyous disbelief.

Step 3: On an August morning, quiver with goosebumps as you smile for photos on the windswept North Wall Quay, outside the tilted glass cylinder of the Irish Convention Centre. 'Naturalisation' will sound like a process involving dairy products. Buy a red body-wrap dress for the Irish Citizenship Ceremony (the dress will be slightly too clingy, so you will spend much of the day holding your breath). After two hours of sitting and standing, dozens of sweaty handshakes, an oath of fidelity to the nation and a flimsy certificate in a plastic sleeve, you should drink five pints of Guinness in The Quays and ask your father-in-law to teach you Irish. He will rub his speckled head and say, 'Oh geez, Luana ... I wouldn't be a great Irish speaker now, sorry.'

Tottering in your strappy silver heels, approach Séan's sister and ask her if she could help you learn Irish. She will shake her shaggy blonde fringe into her pinot grigio and say, 'Ach, Luana, pet, I'd love to help you but I wouldn't have a fuckin' notion about Irish.'

Undeterred, ask Séan to teach you. He will hoot, 'Are you serious? That's hilarious, babe. Sure my Gaelic's brutal. *Cáca. Milséan. Banana.* That's all I'd remember. Fuck, it'd be nearly impossible for a ... for someone from a ...'.

How do you say 'foreigner' in Irish?

On the opposite side of the River Liffey, queue with Gabriela outside the immigration office on Burgh Quay in the washed-out light of 6 a.m. You will have agreed to accompany your friend to renew her visa because she says her English is shit and she needs you to translate. Ask her, 'Gabi, how am I meant to learn Irish when hardly any Irish people can even speak it?'

Gabriela will exhale cigarette smoke, her nose-ring glittering. 'Languages are weird, Luana. You know Irish is partly derived from Sanskrit?' Gabriela studied linguistics in Rio de Janeiro, but here in Dublin she shovels French fries into cardboard boxes for the minimum wage. You know your friend too well to ask her how this happened.

Step 4: Receive a call from Scoil Mhuire National School at 8:45 on a September morning. 'Aisling Burke's waters are after breaking early,' a mewing voice will tell you, 'we've a nine-month maternity post. It's short notice, but if you could come in today ...?'

You now have a job. And you have seven months left in which to learn Irish. Kid yourself that watching *Ros na Rún* whilst lounging on the bed nibbling popcorn counts as a learning exercise, when in fact you're just dozing and reading the English subtitles. Switch the language on your phone into Irish (this will piss you off after a few days; change it back). Dye your hair Temptress Amber. Sign up for Weekly Irish Conversation Exchange at O'Donoghue's Lounge, where a man with veiny cheeks and rheumy eyes will lead you away from the other Irish speakers for a 'beginner session' in a shadowy corner of the pub. He will lean close enough for you to smell his oniony breath, and his beer belly will brush your thigh as he asks '*tá tú singil?*' Leave early, forgetting your umbrella. Hurry into a sheet of rain, which will close up behind you, like the beaded curtain on your mama's kitchen door.

Enrol in Irish For Beginners at the Scoil Ghaeilge on Dame Street. Classes should begin on an October evening sweet with the fragrance of rotting leaves. Most of your classmates will be Irish retirees in search of a new hobby. If they gawk at you and ask why the feck a Brazilian girl like you is learning Gaelic, explain that you are a primary teacher with a master's in education from São Paulo University, you moved here to Ireland because you fell in love with an Irish man, and that you must learn Irish in order to teach at primary level. Notice your classmates' eyes glazing over (at this point you should probably stop speaking). Learn your first phrase in Irish, and enjoy the Gaelic words undulating on your tongue. *Tá tuirse orm*: the tiredness is on me.

Learn 'indigo' in Irish.

Learn 'five hundred and seventy-three' in Irish.

Learn 'broccoli' in Irish.

Realise that at this rate it will take several decades for you to reach the required level of Irish fluency. Purchase a copy of *Is Féidir Linn! Teach Yourself Gaelic*. Inspired by a blue-skied Sunday morning, buy some sheets of brightly coloured cardboard, cut them into uneven squares and write the Irish on one side, the English on the other. Man. *Fear*. Woman. *Bean*. Heart. *Croí*. Break. *Briste*.

How do you ask '*você me ama?*' in Irish?

Turn off the bedside lamp. Kiss Séan's neck and wriggle against him. When he doesn't react, consider flicking the light back on. Say nothing. Perhaps fears are like *fantasmas*; if you don't mention them, then they won't be real. Lie awake in Séan's arms until he rolls over to sleep with his back to you. How long is it since you really looked at each other? Since he really saw you? Feel as if you have woken up into a nightmare and that reality is somewhere ahead of you in your sleep.

Step 5: Tear open another envelope with your teeth, leaving lip-prints of Sherbet Promise lipstick on the blue-lined paper. *A Chara*, an Irish inspector will visit your classroom on 3 November at 11:20 to assess the first stage of the *Scrúdú le hAghaidh Cáilíochta sa Ghaeilge*. In order to fulfil this stage of the assessment, you must teach a lesson using ONLY IRISH. *Má úsáideann an t-iarrthóir aon Bhéarla, ní bheidh de chead ag an scrúdaitheoir marc níos airde ná 2.5 as 6 a bhronnadh* (ANY use of English will cap your mark at 40 per cent).

Panic. With the help of Google Translate, write out your entire thirty-minute Irish lesson like a badly plotted film script.

Shake hands with a tall grey-haired man in a green reindeer jumper and mutter an embarrassed '*Dia duit, conas atá tú?*' You will not understand his reply. He will take out his black clipboard and sit at the back of your classroom, almost doubled over on one of the yellow-legged infant-sized chairs.

Take a deep breath and give a fumbling lesson on *an aimsir*, during which Fionn will decide to steal Nabil's Spider-Man pencil case. In retaliation, Nabil will trap Fionn's index finger between two desks. Meanwhile, Belal will take a pair of plastic-handled scissors and hack Hamza's fringe off, and Beatrice will tug on your skirt and wail, 'Teacher! Agnieszka she say some bad word for me in Polish!' Attempt to resolve these disputes without using a word of English. Orchestrate an impromptu game of *Céard atá sa Mhála?* Rally the children into a song about a duck up a tree, which has absolutely no connection to the lesson you are meant to be teaching. At this point, thirty-two sets of small eyes will be regarding you with quizzical expressions.

Switch back into English as soon as the inspector leaves. Remind your class to 'keep your hands and your feet and your unkind words to yourself'. Your control over the class of six-year-olds should now be slipping through your fingers like a fistful of sand. Feel miniscule as a *tartaruguinha* being swept across oceans by the tsunami of the children's noise.

Following this sharp peak in noise level, you should be summoned to an after-school meeting with Mrs O'Reilly. The principal will pour you a cup of milky tea, pat her mousy bob and fold her hands in the lap of her floral skirt. 'Ms Silva, tell me, how are you finding the class?' Her tapered smile will not reach her pencil-grey eyes.

Mumble, 'Okay … not too bad I guess.'

Mrs O'Reilly will sip her tea, 'Look, Luana, we're here to help you, pet. I know how difficult it can be, but the noise from your class this afternoon was through the roof. Through. The. Roof.' Nod mutely, to which she will continue, 'Now, perhaps you just need more support? Now I've noticed your class has less Class Stars than any other class in Scoil Mhuire, Luana. It would be great to change this, wouldn't it?'

Smile and gulp your tea. Part your lips, but find no words emerging. Contemplate robbing some Class Stars off another class's display board.

Step 6: Call Séan to tell him about your inspection. If he doesn't answer, phone his bandmate John, who will tell you,

'Sorry Luana, umm … there was no Drifters rehearsal this evening.'

Say, 'Oh yeah, of course. It's Tuesday. Silly me.' Hang up. Blood will pound in your ears for a few minutes, making you feel as if you have gone temporarily deaf.

Stand by the stove stirring black-bean rice. Later, you will hear Séan's metal-capped boots stomping up the stairs, and the discordant strum of him retuning his guitar. When he plods into the kitchen, ask, 'So how was the rehearsal tonight?'

He will tell you, 'It was grand, yeah.'

Feijoada should now be simmering in the pot, fogging up the dark window. The warm air should be heavy with moisture, as if you were trapped in the entrails of the Mata Atlântica rainforest. While he speaks to you, Séan's narrow eyes will flit between the bubbling beans and the pearly buttons of your blouse. Experience for the first time the sensation of missing someone when they are standing right in front of you.

Step 7: Dye your hair Cocoa Velvet. Make sure you wear the black silk dress with the low-cut neckline to the Rootless Drifters' Christmas gig at The Bleeding Rose. (Your husband will tut at your cleavage and will say, 'Fuck sake, Luana, do you have to be so … so … so Brazilian?') John will pat your back and ask, 'Luana! I heard you're learning Irish. That's unreal. How's it going?' Tell him that you are progressing excellently and are now borderline fluent. If Séan then strides over and introduces the new bass player, Áine, who is a fluent Irish speaker, you should avoid her chirpy questions and feign indigestion. Leave Séan at the gig and hail a taxi home.

Slam the front door shut, hurl your red handbag across the room and twist open your last bottle of cachaça. Take a gulp of the clear liquid, which scalds a trail from your oesophagus to the pit of your stomach. Try to drink yourself into a place beyond thinking.

Open your sticky eyes five hours later, your clammy cheek plastered to the leather sofa. Wipe the spidery trails of mascara gloop from your eyelashes, and realise that Séan has not come home. Around your fence, blue LED icicle lights will blink at you sadly. Waking up will feel like a feat of extreme survival.

Butter your toast, and use the knife to slit open another letter, leaving trails of marmalade on the envelope. '*A Chara,* as a result of your classroom inspection, you have passed the teaching aspect of the *Scrúdú le hAghaidh Cáilíochta sa Ghaeilge.* As the next step of your Irish Language Requirement, you must complete a residential study period in the Irish-speaking Gaeltacht.'

Google 'Gaeltacht courses for primary teachers'. Book to spend a week at Coláiste Loch Con Nualla in Connemara during February half-term break.

Step 8: Whisper a prayer to São Cristóvão as you scrape the snow from your windscreen. Séan will watch from the doorway while you cram the boot of your Micra. Pack the fluffy blue Foxford your mother-in-law gave you, an AA road map, a backpack bulging with woolly sweaters, *Is Féidir Linn,* a three-pack of notebooks, your green stormproof coat, a Tupperware box of *pão de queijo* from Gabriela and your last packet of Fandangos crisps. He will fold his arms and mutter, 'Fuckin' ridiculous … how the hell d'ya think you're going to learn Irish, babe …? Waste of money … probably get lost anyway … stupid fuckin' idea.'

Click the boot shut and throw your arms around his neck. 'I'll miss you.'

He will pull away and mutter, 'For God's sake, Luana, mind out for black ice.' Notice the coldness of his ferret-like eyes, the fact that he's wearing a Rootless Drifters T-shirt embossed with a logo of his own face, and the girlishness of his hand with its long guitar-strumming nails. Wonder why you never heeded these things before. Love and hate morph with the suddenness of a São Paulo nightfall.

Programme your Path-Finder98 and head west on the M4, through the flat expanse of the midlands. Bypass Galway city and continue through the outlying towns of Moycullen and Oughterard. Turn off the main Clifden Road onto a narrow, winding track signposted 'The Gaeltacht'. Follow the road as it weaves and curves around every ditch in the bog, but do not pay too much attention to the road directions you were given by the secretary at Coláiste Loch Con Nualla. These directions will not take you anywhere near the place you are trying to reach.

After two hours driving in desperate circles around the wilds of county Galway, realise that your destination isn't even on the map. Disconnect your Path-Finder98 and shove it into the glove compartment. As daylight fades, get out of your car and slam the door. Your breath will fog in the freezing air. Shout at a few uninterested sheep. Sense the hostile glare of this grey-green land in which you will forever be a foreigner. Cover your face with your hands. Remember the country you left behind. Ilha de Anchieta, where big-eyed spider monkeys perform acrobatics in the palms. Waves crashing on the soft white sand of Caraguatatuba. Your mama's hands. All of this you abandoned for a love as fleeting as quickly browning açai blossoms. Pick up a rock and sling it into the mutilated darkness of the bog.

Get back into your car. Your bluish hands will be shivering on the steering wheel. How do you say *'perdido'* in

Irish? Kiss your *sorte* necklace. Do a U-turn and judder back up the potholed limestone track. A snow-blotched sheet of bog will stretch for miles before it creases around the edges of the Atlantic. Yellow wind bushes will be bright splashes on the tawny landscape. Gnarled branches of hawthorn trees will lean sideways as if caught in a perpetual storm. Locate the whitewashed farmhouse just as darkness has begun to drape across the rugged shoulders of the Loch Con Nualla hills.

Step 9: You should be greeted by a small blonde woman in a leopard-print apron. 'Come on in pet, I'm Mary, your *Bean an tí*. I'll not make you speak Irish now, not to worry. You're from Brazil? My son's over there travelling, so he is.'

Follow her into a furnace-warm kitchen and find ten pairs of primary-teacher eyes staring at you like rows of politely seated orcs. Listen to ten names. Forget all of them. Accept a cup of milky tea and a slice of buttered soda bread. Feel an avalanche of exhaustion bury you when the other students ask why a Brazilian girl like yourself is learning Irish. Tell them 'I don't know why I'm learning this stupid language at this stage'. Some of the women will titter, perhaps unsure whether you are joking or not. Stupid *vacas*. Curse at them in your head in your crudest São Paulo slang. Duck your head away from their curious glances and swill your lukewarm tea.

Leave the kitchen and tiptoe into the dormitory. Undress. Lie on your assigned bunk bed and peep out through a chink in the threadbare curtains. The moonlit loch will be windswept into a texture like ruffled velvet. Shiver uncontrollably, despite your thermal pyjamas, Wilderness Explorer sleeping bag and fluffy blue Foxford. Consider getting out of bed to put on your woolly hat and gloves, but become paralysed by the leaden inertia of dreams. Think of Séan. Imagine that your bed is a raft that has been cut adrift, and that you will float forever without reaching the shores of this night.

Step 10: Attend lessons in the sea-facing classroom of Coláiste Loch Con Nualla from nine to five each day, but do not expect to understand a word the teacher, Kathleen, says. A wild-haired woman from the Aran Islands with a hooked nose and drawn-on eyebrows, Kathleen will not write anything on the dusty pine-green board, but will sit in a creaking armchair and reel off Irish sentences like incantations. '*Déarfainn* ... *déarfá* ... *déarfadh sélsí* ... *déarfaimis* ... *déarfadh sibh* ... *déarfaidís* ...'. Try to make some notes, but find yourself unable to do this because you cannot spell anything in Irish. Sneak out your mobile under the desk and try to google 'spelling patterns in Irish', but find that there is no internet signal in Loch Con Nualla. Tears should sting, making your eyeliner bleed.

While waves of Gaelic roll over your head, look out of the tall windows at the lunar landscape, across which dry stone walls are slung like broken rosary beads. Study a century of black-and-white school photos patchworking the rough stone walls, and try to envisage what it would be like to grow up out here, so far from everywhere. Think about the phrase 'non-national', and imagine yourself as a seed lifting on a chaotic breeze and drifting away from your home place, never to return.

Crunch back up the frosty hill towards your *Bean an tí*'s farmhouse. Stop at a rusty gate to feed tufts of long, wet grass to two earth-brown donkeys, their hairy lips tickling your palm. 'Gorgeous, aren't they?' A square-jawed woman with turf-brown curls will stop beside you, rolling up the sleeves of her peacock-blue coat. 'So, are ye in Ireland long?' she'll ask as she pats the smaller donkey's tufty black mane.

'Eight years, almost. I came here for one year to learn English, but you know …'.

'Met a fella was it? Always the way. I'm Caoimhe.'

'Luana.'

Walk together up the rest of the hill in comfortable silence, past where an old red fishing boat is marooned on a bed of heather.

In the kitchen, Mary will be serving dinner. Douse your tasteless breaded chicken and over-boiled carrots in salt and pepper whilst zoning in and out of the teachers' loud conversation. 'So, you're from Ballinasloe?' 'Do you know Deirdre Fallon, the sister of Padraic and Séamus …?' 'When we were above, doing the Leaving …'. 'Tell me now, would they be related to the McFaddens from Oughterard … used to go with my cousin's friend …?'

Once they have all gone to bed, sit at the kitchen table and copy passages from *Is Feidir Linn* into your looping handwriting. The only sound should be the scratch of your biro nib, the fingernail-drum of sleet on the window and the gurgle of the kettle on the cherry-red Aga.

Like salt crystallising on summer-beach skin, or the solidifying whites of poached eggs on a Sunday morning, begin to find patterns emerging from the embryonic mess of the Irish language. Nod with satisfaction when Kathleen tells you that the answers you've given to the *Modh Coinníollach* questions are spot-on. Start to formulate simple sentences in Irish, and whisper these to yourself. *Luana Paula is ainm dom. Táim naoi mbliana is fiche d'aois. Is as Brasaíl ó dhúchas mé, ach táim i mo chónaí i mBaile Átha Cliath anois.*

Step 11: On your final night in Loch Con Nualla, link your arm with Caoimhe's to steady yourselves along the frosty lane. Watch the two brown donkeys trot into the village past the fogged-up window of McDonagh's. Spot the same two weary-looking donkeys plodding back up the road by themselves two hours later, as if returning from a night on the tiles. Drink pints of Guinness until you lose count of them. Sip your first shot of Jameson. Down your second shot.

Follow a trail of laughter up the country road into darkness so tangible it should have a texture, a smell, a taste. This is the first time in your life you have experienced the real Irish night, away from the murky dishwater of the city sky. Explain this to Caoimhe. She will nod sincerely, although you have been speaking in Portuguese for the last ten minutes. Crawl into your bunk bed just as a pale yolk of sun rises over Loch Con Nualla.

Hand Kathleen a cheque for €1,200 for your stay in the Gaeltacht, and wonder if you will have to sell half of your internal organs to pay for the luxury of learning this language. Swap numbers with Caoimhe, who will hug you and say, 'Good luck, missus. See you in the exam.'

Drive back up the winding road, and watch the Connemara hills retreating in your rear-view mirror until the imposing mountains are nothing more than purplish fingerprints smudged along the horizon. Follow the M4 back across the belly of Ireland, sketching a line from one coast to the other. Three hours later, enter the grey outskirts of Dublin feeling as if you are resurfacing from the swamps of a hallucination.

Step 12: When you pull into your driveway, Séan will be leaning on his Vespa with his wispy hair veiling his eyes. Under his leather jacket he'll still be wearing the Rootless

Drifters T-shirt with the logo of his face on it. As you approach you will notice the khaki backpack on the Vespa behind him. He will put a hand on your arm. 'Luana, I've been thinking. Fuck it, it's just ... with the new tour coming up ... I just need some time to ...'.

Shake your head, 'No, no, no, no.' Step into his arms and bury your head against the shoulder of his jacket. His sandalwood aftershave will take you back to the night you met, when his first touch evoked a type of muscle-memory, as if your body already knew him from a previous life. You already had your flight to Sâo Paulo booked, but your plans to leave Ireland dissolved the minute Séan first hugged you. You sensed your future dividing like the Parnaíba River Delta, splintering into different paths.

Séan will pull back, taking both your hands in his. 'Luana, please ... it's just for a few weeks, just till I get my head around ...'.

How do you say 'stop talking' in Irish?

There are no words you could possibly say to Séan, in English, Irish or Portuguese. Stand in the doorway and listen to his bike chortling down the cobbled pathway of the home you once loved. After the snarl of his Vespa has faded into a whisper, watch a fuzzy rainbow leak through a slate-grey sky. At this moment it should be sunny somewhere on the horizon, but it will start raining where you are.

Close the door. Draw your green living room curtains, which will fill the room with sub-aquatic shadows. Sit cross-legged in the epicentre of a grief that is every human emotion distilled down to 100 per cent proof. If your mama calls you, do not answer your phone.

Step 13: Teach. Sometimes you will need the distraction provided by your class of infants far more than they need you.

'Teacher, he hit me!' 'Teacher, my nose is itchy!' 'Teacher, she won't be my friend!' Through the eyes of your assembled six-year-olds, see yourself not as a broken wanderer but as a Fixer of All Things. On yard duty, try to keep check on the dizzying rush of children, an enterprise as pointless as attempting to patrol a hurricane. Pupils will swerve around the yard, haphazardly bright in their winter coats, like escaped pieces of a Cubist painting. 'I speak Arabic.' Nabil will skip up to tell you, his black fringe mad in the wind. Ask him 'How do you say hello?' Repeat after him. 'You're not exactly saying it properly, teacher,' he will smile.

After a rainy playtime, a type of mass captivity-induced hysteria will ensue. The children carry a constricted energy: flushed cheeks, scrambling, elbow-butting, pencil-fighting. In the midst of this chaos, you should attempt to conduct the daily Irish lesson. *Gorm … Dorcha … Bándearg … Buí….* Mrs O'Reilly will stick her mousy-brown bob around the door and say, 'Oh how lovely, Ms Silva. I didn't realise you were teaching them Portuguese.'

Step 14: Read the next letter without translating it. Swallow hard. *A Chara*, your final examinations for the *Scrúdú le hAghaidh Cáilíochta sa Ghaeilge* will take place on Tuesday April 7 between 10:00 and 13:00.

You now have fewer than six weeks left. You will lose your Teaching Council Registration if you do not pass. Panic. Sit at your dusty dining room table surrounded by toppled-over towers of Irish flashcards, mugs of whitish congealing tea, biscuit wrappers and stacks of dog-eared Irish notes. Over the wall, graveyard daffodils should bop their heads in the March breeze. 'Why don't you just give up and get a different job?' Gabriela will say. 'You don't even like primary teaching, Luana. Why not just quit?' Shake your head. How do you say in Irish 'I cannot give up now'? Run your hands over your face. Grit your teeth. Open a new chapter of *Is Féidir Linn*.

Listen to Kathleen giving free Irish lessons on Skype. During these lessons, you should contemplate:

Smashing the screen of the laptop against the bedroom wall.

Calling Séan.

Returning to São Paulo, where at least you wouldn't have to learn Irish.

Do not attempt actually to learn Irish or to write essays in Irish. If, spurred by a blast of hormonal enthusiasm, you happen to write an essay in Irish and email it to Kathleen, she will reply within ten minutes telling you 'It's complete crap, Luana,' and she will scold you for using Google Translate. Embrace the art of cramming. Read group emails from Caoimhe and the other Loch Con Nualla students (they are now placing bets on which essay question will come up). With blind faith, rote-learn the essays Kathleen has emailed you. Pray to every deity you know that Kathleen's predicted essay questions will come up.

Google 'fastest way to learn a new language'. Find out that the human brain is most likely to recall the information it receives immediately before sleep. Keep your Irish flashcards and rote-learned essays on your bedside table, and study them until your eyelids droop. Sleep. In your dreams, Portuguese, Irish and English should now be merging into one language. Dream of seven skewered chicken hearts cooking in the *churrasco* flames. In this dream, you will be standing on the roof of your mama's building in Moema, and Séan will approach you from behind, pushing you close to the skyscraper's edge. Wake up alone in your double bed. Stare at the ceiling while you figure out which set of sounds to speak.

Step 15: Sit at desk number thirty-eight and stare at the exam booklet.

SCRÚDÚ LE hAGHAIDH CÁILÍOCHTA SA GHAEILGE – PÁIPÉAR I – 100 MARC
Trí huaire an chloig don pháipéar seo (10:00 – 13:00).
Cúig cheist le freagairt, ceann amháin as gach Roinn.

Write 'Luana Paula de Silva O'Connor' into the empty box using a running-out blue biro, so that the last letters of your married name are carved into the crisp white sheet. Caoimhe, wearing a canary-yellow cardigan, will give you a fingers crossed from across the room.

Feel a lump like hot *pão de queijo* in your throat when you open the booklet and see Kathleen's chosen essay question on the first page. Grip your *sorte* necklace. Regurgitate Kathleen's entire essay by heart as best you can. Have a guess at some of the other questions. Resist the urge to pass comment when two Irish girls stroll out of the *Triail Chluastuisceana* saying, 'That was easy wasn't it?' Do not shout 'IT'S VERY BLOODY FUCKING EASY IF YOU WERE BORN AND BRED IN IRELAND, ISN'T IT???!' Feel your cheeks flush. How do you say 'Dear God, please help me' in Irish?

In the *Scrúdú Béil*, listen to your Converse creak across the shadowy expanse of the exam room. Sit down at a mahogany table opposite two old men with greyish whiskers protruding from their noses. Watch them demonstrate with great pride the device they will use to record your speaking: a machine that seems to have been resurrected from the 1960s. Don't give in to the urge to laugh hysterically at this point (it's just the lack of sleep). Listen to the old men's questions, and answer in Irish as best you can. You should be half-aware that you are throwing in the odd word of Portuguese. Hope that they don't notice. *Luana Paula is ainm dom …*

Chuaigh mé go dtí an Ghaeltacht ar feadh um semana. Bhí bean an tí an-deas. Bhí sí tipo agus flaithiúil.

After the exams, traipse down the hill to The Winding Road with Caoimhe and the other teachers. Drink two pints of Guinness and feel the tiled floor of the smoking area become as unstable as a sheet of melting ice. By now your head should be throbbing, your body drained and limp as a fallen leaf.

Slightly tipsy, call Séan and invite him to the pub. When he arrives and hands you a bunch of pursed-lipped daffodils, avoid his eyes. Stand by his side, swaying slightly. If he stares at you and says, 'Luana, please ... can we at least talk ...?' shake your head. If he tries to kiss you under the glow of an outdoor heater, duck away.

Gabriela will then turn up, pinching your waist from behind. 'Luana! What's this text about leaving Ireland? You can't leave! What will I do if you leave?'

'You're leaving?' The amber orbs in Séan's pond-water eyes will blur. 'Fuck, Luana, don't tell me you're fuckin' leaving?' Before you can answer, he will hug you tightly. Clasped in the bony warmth of his arms, your cheek pressed against his skull tattoo, a familiar darkness will gather inside you. A grainy blackness like coffee granules filtered through the stuff of days, building up as toxic sediment in the pit of your stomach. Swallow hard as a gritty feeling rises in your mouth. Push away from Séan, run past Gabriela, scurry into the Ladies, lock a cubicle door behind you and throw up into a toilet bowl. Rip off a sheet of loo roll and wipe the trail of watery vomit from your chin. Run your hands through the undyed roots of your knotty hair. *Santa Maria Mãe de Deus.*

Duck between elbows and out of the pub before either Gabi or Séan has a chance to see you. Newly arrived swallows will be skydiving across the bright spring evening. Take a shortcut home through Glasnevin Cemetery. Kneel and trace one of the granite inscriptions with your finger. *I líonta Dé go dtugtar sinn.* May we be brought into God's nets. The circle-headed headstones will eye you with curiosity, and a rat will scurry across your path from under one of the yews. Jog home through the bitter yew-berried evening, lock your purple door and throw yourself onto your squeaky leather sofa. Don't worry if you do not understand why you're crying at this moment; you're not meant to.

Step 16: Wait. From the window of a Boeing 747, watch Dublin retreat beneath a torn veil of clouds, until the houses of your adopted city are so small you could scoop them up and fit them into your pocket. Spend the Irish summer at home in São Paulo, where it is winter. Refuse to talk to your mama about what happened with Séan.

Shut your bedroom door and stay in your room watching reruns of *Esperança* and listening to old Djavan songs on YouTube. *'Mais fácil aprender japonês em braile ... do que você decidir se dá ou não ...'.* By now, the switch in seasons will have given you a head-cold. Your mama will pour all of her concern for you into her *feijoada*, and the smoky black-bean taste will catch in your throat. Take the elevator up to the rooftop at sundown to see the skyscrapers lit up like lanterns. Watch the shifting geometry of the São Paulo skyline and wonder why your birth city no longer feels like home.

Little things should now irritate you about São Paulo: the morning smog that chokes the canyons of Moema, the gaudy bombardment of advertising on the privatised Globo TV channels and the power cuts that frequently blinker the city for whole afternoons. You've lost your taste for *pão de queijo*, and *coxinha* seems too salty. Spend hours wandering around the city alone, circling the glassy lake of Parque Iberapuera, on which languid black swans drift. Google 'resettling in home country after living abroad', but this search will only provide information for rehomed asylum seekers. Spot a Tourism Ireland advert on a flickering billboard in a shopping centre outside Santos: three freckled children grinning against a purple-hilled backdrop. Freeze at the top of an escalator, felled by sudden emotion.

July will slide into August, and your mama will stop asking you when you're returning to Ireland. Celebrate your thirtieth birthday with a surprise *churrasco* on the terrace. As the pale winter sun slips into the collar of the skyscrapers, pour another cup of milky tea and retell your mama the story of how you attempted to learn Irish. Already your life in Ireland will feel like a dream recounted by somebody else. Draft five emails to Séan, and abandon all of them. How do you say 'I'm lost' in Irish? How do you say 'I'm confused' in Irish? How do you say how you really feel in any language?

Step 17: Lock yourself in your mama's bathroom and scrutinise the creased white envelope in your hands. On the now-familiar logo, the Salmon of Knowledge will leap through a square of cobalt-blue. Lean your head against the sun-bleached wallpaper. Imagine the worn-out tendrils of the fleur-de-lis weaving into your honey-brown hair and rooting you to this place. Try to formulate a single sentence that will express the meaning of your eight years in Ireland. Close your eyes. Take a deep breath. Kiss your *sorte* necklace and wonder what your papa would make of all this. Rip open the envelope with shaking hands.

Fling the bathroom door open and shout out 'Mama, guess what!'

Kamikaze Love

Oisín knows there is something in his bedroom, but he's not quite sure if it's me. He stands naked from his bed. Outside, it is raining. 'Fucksake,' he mutters, seeing the rain. From the bed, I study Oisín as he searches for his shorts. *Kon kon chicki chin*, the soft rain whispers as it dribbles on the roof. *Kon kon chicki chin*, my friends and I used to sing as the dragon shimmered though the checkerboard streets of Kyôto. All through the night we would beat our drums, *kon chicki chin*, praying for it to rain. But mostly, here in Dublin, people pray for the rain to stop. When the sun is shining, Irish people smile and say, '*GRANDDAY, THANKSBETOGOD!*' But when it's raining, all the Irish people look so sad.

On Oisín's shoulders, the constellation of freckles shows *Orihime* and *Hikoboshi* meeting in the Milky Way. 'I'd best be heading,' he mutters to himself as he pulls on his grey hoody and wrestles into the arms of his coat. He rubs his patchy beard, ruffles his too-long hair, and frowns at the bed one more time before he leaves the room. For a second, his eyes focus on the space where my belly button is. Oisín always used to linger when I was unclothed like this, with my long black hair on the pillow, but he cannot see me now.

PUT BINS OUT OISÍN says a note on the kitchen counter of the attic apartment Oisín and Donal share. This week Donal has gone home to Cork, and Oisín has proceeded to make a kip of the place, although Donal asked him not to. 'You've gotta get a grip, man,' Donal said before he went away. I know this word: grip. It means holding on to something very tightly. But what? Oisín doesn't have anything to hold on to. Oisín crumples Donal's note and throws it into the overflowing bin. He slams the door behind him. From the window, I watch the gangly shape of Oisín striding the slate-wet street. He is meant to be going to college, but he hasn't been to any lectures or tutorials for the last three weeks. Overdue library books are stacked on his desk, and his handwritten essay on *Whether there are Universal Moral Principles that are Right for all Persons and at all Times* has not progressed any further down the blue-lined page. Watching from above, I can see that something in his walk has changed since I've been gone. I think it will not change back.

I just need to delete my message from Oisín's phone, and then I can leave this place. Every day I've been coming back here, trying to delete that text. But as usual, he has taken his phone with him in the pocket of his baggy blue jeans. Now I will have to follow him out of his house and into the rain to try to delete my text. *Fucksake.*

The rain in Ireland is not only vertical, but horizontal and diagonal too. Sometimes the rain even comes upwards off the street, so you do not know which way the rain is falling. The Irish rain gets angry if you try to use an umbrella. The wind grabs your umbrella's handle and turns your umbrella inside-out. Luckily, I do not need an umbrella these days.

I follow Oisín around the city centre, past the pointing needle and all the statues of Irish heroes from the past.

Irish people like *The Past*, I think. With Oisín I watched an Irish movie about *The Past* once. The movie was about two brothers fighting because of Ireland's independence from England. One man in this movie was crying. I did not know why. When the movie finished, Oisín said, 'So, what did you make of that, Anju? I have to admit it's one of my favourites. Brilliant film, isn't it?'

I said 'Yes, it was very interesting,' but I thought I would not like to see that movie again. My *chichi* told me I must not speak about the war because at this time we lost many things. 'Kamikaze' was the most forbidden word in our house. If I spoke about the war, my family would not have forgiven me for this.

Oisín turns off Grand Canal Street, and I follow him into a tall red building with a gold-plated plaque by the door. A small woman behind a big desk asks Oisín his name, and then she shows him through another door. The next room is dark and full of cats. I can hear the soft pad of their paws along the bookshelves. One of these cats can sense me, and its black tail writhes and twists like an angry *mamushi*.

'How are you today, son?' An old man indicates a chair by the window, and Oisín sits down.

'I don't know.' He stares at his hands. 'Some days I feel fine, almost like it never happened. Then I'll realise I haven't thought about Anju for a few hours. And then I'll end up feeling more guilty than ever. It's just a vicious cycle.' He sniffs and rubs his nose. 'Sorry.'

The old man offers him a pink-patterned tissue from a box. 'All this is still very recent, Oisín. You've suffered a major trauma. What you're experiencing is normal. It's just going to take more time.'

Oisín blows his nose. He's quiet for a minute, looking at his hands. 'It's just … it's more than that. I mean, I feel so guilty, and there's that aspect to it. But then sometimes I feel as if she's actually *here*. As if she's following me around or something. I know this sounds insane, but have you any experience with the paranormal? I mean, you must deal with bereaved people all the time. Has anyone ever mentioned anything like this?'

'Well, there are various ways in which grief can manifest itself …'.

This is becoming boring, so I go outside.

It is still raining. I float into the white haze of rain and along the sky-coloured road. Near the bus shelter, three Irish children are splashing in the puddles with their flapping winter jackets bright as toys. I used to have a job in Dublin looking after small Irish children like this. I was an au pair for two children called Michael and Siobhán. That job did not last very long. 'Look, Anjoooo,' the small boy, Michael, greeted me one day. 'I lost my tooooof!'

'You are a good boy, Michael,' I told him. He was very cute now with his gap-toothed smile. We went into the garden and we counted, 'One … two … THREE!' I threw Michael's tooth high onto the roof, where it rattled on the tiles. This meant that Michael would have a very strong smile. But Michael started to cry.

'What about the toooof fairyyyyy?' Michael cried.

'What is the tooffairy?' I asked.

'She's the one what brings the five euro!'

Michael cried all afternoon, and when his mother, Síle, came home, she also started to cry. I heard Síle on the phone saying, 'The feckin' foreign au pair's after lobbing Michael's feckin' first tooth on the feckin' roof!' I tried to explain that in Japan this is a special tradition, but Síle was not listening. 'What's wrong with these feckin' foreign au pairs?' Síle cried. I left their house without saying goodbye.

Oisín leaves the tall red building and lights up a cigarette. He pulls up his hood and steps back into the rain, which is shouting down onto a nearby bus stop.

I feel sorry for Oisín. It was not his fault. How was he to know that in Kyôto a boy called Ryo used to live in the student apartment next to mine? Through the walls, I used to imagine him sleeping. Ryo was one year younger than me. He had sad eyes, a wispy goatee and a large Adam's apple that made him seem anxious always. We both studied mathematics at Kyôto University, and in a lecture one day I noticed a fresh cut on Ryo's right arm. I knew that Ryo had made that serpent-tongue cut by himself. When the lecture had finished, I took the train home with Ryo and invited him into my apartment.

'I'm a loose cannon, Anju,' Ryo said when we first put our faces up close. I could smell the flavour of his toothpaste. The fresh sweat under his T-shirt. The coconut oil on his hair. 'I might hurt you, Anju ... I'm not normal. You'd better stay away.' I shook my head and put my young face closer to Ryo's. I shut my eyes and kissed him. And later, I tried to keep the memory of that kiss preserved; a perfect frozen moment from a dream.

In Ireland you must answer each question with another question. '*HOWAREYA?*' Oisín's friend Tom asks him.

'*HOWAREYA?*' Oisín replies.

'Let me buy you a pint, man,' Tom says. He avoids looking at Oisín's bloodshot eyes. Tom goes to the bar and Oisín sits with his phone on the table. Maybe I could sneak inside his phone now and delete my text. I'm getting very close to the phone when Tom returns to the table with two tall glasses. Many Irish people buy black liquid when they want to speak about something. 'Cheers.' Oisín takes a gulp.

'Listen, man, can I ask you something? You're going to think this is really weird.'

'Go for it,' Tom says.

'Right, well, don't get freaked out, but have you ever heard of anyone being haunted? Like a poltergeist or something like that?'

'Sure,' Tom replies, wiping froth from his upper lip. 'An aunty of mine works in the GPO. She says it's genuinely creepy in there after dark. All sorts of weird noises and things being moved around overnight, like. But hang on … you're not talking about … *Anju?*'

'I'm not sure, man. I don't know. It's just this really weird feeling I've had ever since the funeral. It's as if someone's watching me. You know that feeling you get on the back of your neck when you're being stared at? And then when I got home yesterday, it if was as if someone had been riffling through my stuff. Seriously, there were things everywhere.'

'Burglars, you reckon?'

'I thought that at first,' Oisín says, 'but nothing had been taken. It was mostly just my jeans, flung on the floor with all the pockets turned inside-out.'

'Geez.' Tom inflates his cheeks and exhales slowly. 'I mean, it could happen. I definitely wouldn't rule it out. What else?'

'Well, there are these marks on my back …'. He starts to lift his T-shirt.

Tired of their conversation, I drift over the wall and along the beachfront, where there are many trees with their branches swept sideways. 'I came to Ireland because of the hawthorn bushes, the *sanzashi*,' I told Oisín when we first met, and he laughed, as if hawthorn bushes were the craziest reason for doing anything. But there are worse reasons for doing things. Or, more often, there are no reasons at all.

There was no reason why I moved in with Ryo, but once it had happened it was done. Every minute we should have been studying we would spend under the duvet, watching movies on his laptop or curled up on our futon playing chess. All the equations we should have been solving slid out through our ears. And for a while, Ryo seemed almost happy. Only in his sleep he'd often jolt and shudder, as if he were falling. Many nights I'd lie awake with my breasts pressed against Ryo's back, keeping a vigil over his dreams.

The rain has eased, and there is a thin man on the beach with a white dog that is barking. The dog wants the man to do something, but the man does not understand the dog's message. This man is able to see me because the dog is dead, and the man's wife is also dead, and so the man has started to follow them into the in-between. *'HOWAREYA?'* The man says to me, 'Don't mind him,' pointing to the dog.

'He is a nice dog,' I tell the man.

'He's a bleedin' terror, so he is. Go fetch!' The man hurls a stick towards the distant water. The dog tears down the wet sand. Upside-down in his reflection, another dog is running too.

'Are you long gone?' the man asks me.

'Three weeks,' I reply.

'Depression, was it?'

'No, it was heartbreak.'

'You're better off so.'

Night is coming, and across the dark water those candy-striped towers have started winking to each other. 'Goodbye,' I say to the man with the dead dog.

The man says, 'Mind yourself, pet.'

The samurai believed you must die falling forwards, never falling back. In the email that Ryo sent me from his smartphone in the seconds before he jumped onto the tracks, he said he was saving his family from the disgrace of his poor grades. I was in my parents' apartment when I got Ryo's email. I did not wait for the news to break, or for the hot feeling to reverberate any further than my chest. I locked myself in the bathroom. Butterfly wings sliced a *seppuku* in my belly, disembowelling my emotions, whispering a way out. The girl in the mirror watched as I slit the first incision into the electric-blue junction on her wrists. Curtains of black hair narrowed her face. She didn't look away.

My *chichi* found me by smashing down the bathroom door. And as I lay bleeding, the only thought that came to me was that the door was damaged. The brass hinge had buckled. The pine panels, on which my *haha* had recorded my height with pencil lines year by year, were splintered now. I thought that someone should fix that door. I worried that nobody would. And as I lay in hospital, drug-induced dreams of Ryo mingled with dreams of that damaged door, which was laddered with the pencil-markings of my height.

Oisín leaves the pub and takes the night-link home. I cuddle up to him on the back seat of the bus, but this time he can feel me and he starts to react. He flinches when I stroke his cheek, and when I try to rub his knotted shoulders he shrugs me away. Soon, other passengers get up discreetly and move to different seats. No one will sit beside Oisín because he's swaying and moaning and slapping his arms to try and get me off him. He finally shouts out, 'Oh my God, would you please leave me alone? Would you just PLEASE get the fuck away from me?!' Other passengers turn to stare, first at Oisín and then at the empty seats around him. He stands and grabs the nearest STOP button on one of the chrome bars, and the bus screeches up to a bus stop. Oisín teeters onto the pavement. With trembling hands, he takes out his lighter and lights up a cigarette.

Dublin tonight is full of voices. A mist is lifting off the Liffey, blurring the city into a watery painting. Oisín is remembering as he walks. He remembers when we first met at the Japanese–English Conversation Exchange in the Ilac Centre Library. Oisín was serious that day. '*Dono yō ni shite iru?*' he asked.

I replied, 'I am fine, thank you.'

For an hour we swapped our words; titbits of conversation we fed to each other. He told me that he had worked in Japan during his gap year, teaching English. 'You speak Japanese very good,' I said. Later that night, Oisín mapped his island for me, pinpointing imaginary cities on my palm. 'Imagine your hand is Ireland, Anju,' he said. 'We're here in Dublin … Cork is here … Galway is here … and this part is the North.' My life-line was the River Shannon, and my heart-line marked the border. He said he would take me all over Ireland to see magic-sounding places. The Cliffs of Mow Hair. The Giant's Cause Way. Lis Towel. Wex Ford. Lim Eric. Ballina Slow.

The first time I met Oisín's friends, they looked at me strangely. 'A Japanese girl?? Ya dark horse!' Tom said when he thought I couldn't understand. The other lads laughed. And I imagined Oisín as a stallion galloping the Dublin streets with the wind in his long black mane. I pulled my sleeves down over my hands while Tom and Oisín's other friends were talking. 'That is a scratch,' I'd told Oisín when he first noticed the white streaks on my wrists, 'I was climbing Mount Fiji.' He believed me: I loved that about him. But I thought that his friends would not so easily believe.

All of this remembering is making Oisín sad. He wipes his eyes and rubs his head. He remembers my black hair and the bright jumpers and leggings I used to wear, making me seem each day like a different-coloured fruit. A lemon jacket. A strawberry hat. Blueberry leggings. A watermelon dress.

'I know it sounds daft, but you're like a doll, Anju. That's what you remind me of, one of those beautiful dolls you see in old Japanese movies,' Oisín remembers telling me on our first date. And I thought of the seven porcelain dolls that used to sit in my parents' window every *Hinamatsuri*; pouting on the red *dansake* over which their silk skirts spread. In ancient days, people used to set those *hina* dolls afloat and send them downriver in Kyôto. Those dolls took all the people's troubles with them. In my head, I saw my family setting me afloat on the grey-green water of the Liffey. I wished I'd had the English words to tell Oisín about this.

'But do you think the language barrier might be a problem, Anju?' Oisín asked me on our second date.

'No,' I said, although I did not know what 'barrier' meant. Later, I looked it up in my electronic dictionary and found it was a type of wall. I imagined then a big wall of words, each brick made out of letters, and Oisín and I trying to climb over it.

Oisín stands outside his apartment and fumbles for his keys. I cannot be arsed waiting for him, so I float through his window instead.

It's so heavy, the silence of this in-between. Time melts and becomes shapeless without the order of days. Without touch, without smell, without taste I float in a body that no longer exists. *Purgatory*, they called it in that painting Oisín and I saw when we ducked into the National Gallery of Ireland to escape the rain one day. In the painting, a man was rowing a boat across a murky river, steering between a place of sunlit meadows and a landscape of fire. Both of these places seemed equally far away, and I noticed the man did not have a very good boat. 'He's in purgatory,' Oisín whispered to me. 'You can see heaven on one side and hell on the other. I've always loved this picture. It's stunning, isn't it?' I nodded, but I felt very sorry for that man in his small boat.

I just need to delete that message, and then I can be free. In his apartment, Oisín is shocked by the cloying reek of the leaking bin bag and the sight of his own mess. On the smoke-yellowed wall is a pure white rectangle, where Oisín's favourite Japanese picture used to hang. He took it down because it reminded him of me, so now the *Great Wave of Kanagawa* faces the wall, its back-rope lolling. Each time Oisín looks at the empty space where the print used to be, he sees the curling tentacles of white waves crashing down.

On a shelf above the sofa is the lavender candle I lit on the last night I was alive in this place. As I blew out the match, I noticed Oisín's eyes avoiding mine. The absence of hope opens up a void in which anything can be said. Later, when the candle was a pool of liquid violet, Oisín put his hand on my naked back and pulled me to him. I whispered '*Aishiteru*' into his shoulder. He froze into a statue, like an Irish hero from *The Past*. I felt his body become as still as death as he translated my words into his.

Oisín takes a bottle of whiskey from the press. All the small glasses are stacked in or around the sink, so he splashes some whiskey into a stolen pint glass. He knocks back the drink and places his two palms on the kitchen counter, as if to stop the world from shaking. His phone is still in his jeans pocket. I float close to him and breathe on his skin. Oisín moans, 'Oh God, what is this?' He digs his hands into his hair. He is really a *drama queen*, but I will miss him when I am gone.

The last night Oisín saw me alive, I waited for him in a café close to Grafton Street. As I waited, I wondered who invented that English phrase *to fall in love*? And how did they know that love is, by definition, an act of falling? Opposite me on the dark café window that night, Oisín's face was in a hurry. His lips did not have time for the words they would speak. His eyes moved quickly around the café, looking at everything but me. 'I feel really bad saying this, Anju, because you're really gorgeous and I've had so much fun with you. But lately I feel it's becoming pretty serious. I feel *responsible* for you, and I just can't handle that. I'm only twenty-four. I'm planning on heading to Australia next year, and I just don't want to get into anything too serious. I'm sorry. Do you know what I mean?'

I nodded, 'Yes, I understand.'

'I mean, you're a great person. Like I said, I just can't commit to this right now; it wouldn't be fair on either of us. Things have got a bit, well, a bit full-on lately.'

'Full-on?' I asked. 'What is "full-on"?'

Oisín sighed and took my hand. 'Full-on means it's too much, Anju. It's just too much. I'm sorry. I hope you don't hate me. I hope we can still be friends?'

I nodded.

'Thanks for being so understanding.'

Oisín kissed my cheek. This kiss was not the same as the kiss he had given me the previous week, and my cheek was not the same either. 'Take care, Anju,' he said, beside a glass-roofed shopping centre.

I watched him walking away.

On my way home, I stopped at O'Reilly's Late Night Pharmacy in Phibsborough, and I bought a pack of razors. No alarm bells rang.

'THANKSAMILLION' the shop assistant said as she handed me my change. As I walked the dark streets home, I saw the strand of black hair that always kicked onto Ryo's forehead. I saw the hazel of Oisín's eyes on Sunday mornings in my bed. In my chest, a hot feeling sliced a *seppuku* in my lungs.

Before I locked the bathroom door, I sent Oisín a text. 'I cannot live without you,' I wrote. Then I took the SIM card from my phone and flushed it down the toilet. There would be no turning back.

Oisín splashes more golden whiskey into the pint glass. He finds three small white candles in a kitchen drawer, lights them and sets them on the counter, then turns out the light. I can see the hairs lifting on his arms, but he breathes steadily and braces himself. 'Right then, Anju, let's try something. I've seen this on those stupid TV shows, so let's see if it works. If you're here, can you manifest yourself? I think we need to talk.'

But I already know what Oisín wants to say. Because of my text, he thinks it's his fault that I arranged the razors in a neat row along the bathtub's edge. He thinks he's to blame that I ran a bath of ice-cold water, yanked off my leggings and sweater, unhooked my bra and dipped my first foot into the cold water, breaking its taut surface. Because of my message, he feels guilty that the water nibbled my toes and up between my legs. He imagines my hair was like black algae floating as I lifted the first blade.

On Oisín's roof, the rain starts up again. This time it's a drum roll. *Kon kon chicki chin! Kon kon chicki chin! Kon*

kon, kon kon, kon kon chicki chin! Oisín drinks more whiskey and places his palms on the counter. He is quite drunk now, but his drunkenness seems to be making him more aware of my presence. 'Anju?' he asks the empty room. 'Anju? Are you there?' His gaze hovers over my naked form. For a second I think he can see me. 'Look, Anju, if you're there, I'm really sorry. I never meant to hurt you. I just didn't think you'd react like that. I mean, God, we'd only been going out for a couple of months and you told me you loved me! *Aishiteru ... I know what that means.* I always knew you were, well, unusual, but I never expected you'd do something so extreme. And if I'm honest ... and you're dead so I may as well be honest ... well I just don't buy it. I don't think you killed yourself because of me; it just doesn't add up. If it wasn't for that stupid text you sent me. Why did you have to do that? Anju, if you're here can you make something move or make a noise or something?'

The room is still. I could swish the curtains or make the candle flames flicker, but I'm too afraid.

'Come ON, Anju,' Oisín shouts. He slams his fist on the counter, and then he holds out both his hands. 'I'm calling you out, all right? If you're here, can you touch my hand? Just touch my hand to show me you're here or SOMETHING.' The room is holding its breath. Oisín pours more whiskey and bangs the bottle down. 'CHRIST! I must be going out of my head.'

He blows out the candles. 'Right, Anju, forget it. Forget it ...'. He pulls off his hoody and staggers towards the bathroom, scattering his clothes in crumpled islands. He leaves his stolen pint glass of whiskey on the cistern lid, turns on the shower, steps into the flow of hot water and sighs. I float into the shower with him and I kiss his lips. I kiss his neck, down to his belly button and down and down and down. Oisín gasps, 'Oh my God.' I am scaring him shitless.

But he doesn't want me to stop. His body trembles. I feel his fear and his desire. 'Oh God.' Oisin leans on the shower wall. 'God.' He trips out of the shower cubicle towards his bed. Half-crying, half-stumbling, he flops onto the mattress. He closes his eyes. 'Christ.'

'TRAGIC SUICIDE OF JAPANESE STUDENT,' the *Evening Herald* said. 'Anju Matsumoto's family in Kyôto have extended their thanks to all the Irish people whose messages of condolence have reached them across the miles ...'.

Those people wrote so many words about me, but they didn't know. That after Ryo had gone, after I was discharged from hospital, and after my white scars had healed, I took a job as a care assistant in a nursing home in Tanabata, a peninsula town far away from Kyôto, on the curve of Ise Bay. The home didn't require qualifications, and they didn't ask any questions. I cleaned bodies, carried laundry, lifted buckets, swept floors, mopped shit and vomit and piss, scrubbed flaking skin, applied cream to bed sores and slept.

And then one day I noticed a framed photograph by the bedside of the oldest resident, Sama Nanako. In the photo, a gnarled and twisted tree carried a shock of wind-blown blossoms. 'It is an Irish tree, a *sanzashi*,' Sama Nanako said. *Hawthorn*. Every morning I studied that picture, and wondered how something so broken could still find strength to bloom. Sama Nanako's cheeks creased into a smile as she handed me the picture. I took it home and placed it on the bookshelf by my bed. I opened a savings account. I googled *Ireland*. For the first time since Ryo had died, I dared to imagine again.

The blade was cold on my wet wrist. One quick press would have been enough to cloud the bathwater red. Under the water, my soft-outlined body belonged to another person. In that moment, I saw hawthorn trees scattering their blossoms, and I felt the shudder of Ryo's restless sleep. I remembered my first summer in Tanabata, when I'd watched people hang their hopes and dreams up from the bamboo, to celebrate the Star Festival when *Orihime* and *Hikoboshi* met. The people of Tanabata wrote their dreams onto small silk flags. By early July, the steaming streets fluttered with the colours of other people's wishes.

And the worst thing about heartbreak, I discovered, is that it heals. It cannot compete with the survival instinct. The appetite for joy. It was with a sense of guilt that I noticed myself healing. Just before July seventh, I permitted myself one small yellow dream, which I hung from the highest bamboo.

自由を願います

I lurched out of the freezing bathtub and I pulled out the plug.

Between my feet, loud water gurgled and streamed off my shivering skin. My teeth chattering, I thought about the text I shouldn't have sent. I knew I must reach Oisín before he had a chance to read my text and panic. I leapt out of the bath. I did not have time to bin the razors or remove the evidence of my intent. I unlocked the bathroom door and tiptoed down the hallway, leaving a trail of dark prints on the deep beige thread. I dried myself, dragged clothes onto my damp skin and stepped outside. I rushed across the main road, mapping a path to where Oisín lived.

'Having failed to slit her wrists, the Japanese girl stepped in front of the number 13,' the *Evening Herald* said.

Finally, I creep into the folds of Oisín's jeans, slip into his phone and find my text. It's easy to get into the black shapes of my words and suck them until they evaporate. As I dissolve my text from Oisín's phone, I can feel myself melt. Tomorrow, he will presume he deleted my text in a drunken fury. In less than a month, he will no longer remember what my message said. He will return the books to the library and put out the bins. He'll start to forgive himself.

Oisín lies naked on his bed.

Outside it is raining.

Just before I vanish, I kiss his forehead and ruffle his long black hair. The rain is finally stopping as he falls into his sleep.

Wild Quiet

U – N – I – C – E – F. Those were the first English letters you learnt how to read. You and Aniya watched those blue letters flapping on a white plastic sheet over your heads. Later, you asked Dad to tell you what those letters said. 'Repeat after me,' Dad said, and he looked almost happy, like how he used to look back home in Mogadishu. You liked the scrambling *kaneeco* shape of English letters, so different from Arabic. Over the next few years in Dadaab, your Dad taught you how to say lots of other things in English. *Hello. My name is. I come from Somalia.* So when the white man with wriggly blue lines in his hand said, 'Hello there,' you were able to say back, 'Hello, my name is Khadra, and this is Aniya.'

'Well, would you listen to that!' The white man said. 'Aren't you the clever-clogs?' And he put a needle into your arm, and it stung like a *kaneeco* bite, and Aniya made big cries, but you didn't cry. Not at all.

Dad stopped teaching you English on the day Aniya was lost.

And today, when the teacher says, 'Hello, Khadra, I'm Miss Murphy, welcome to Bunmaglinty Primary,' you can't think of any words to say. A wind creeps under the classroom window. There are treeless green hills outside, and the black curve of the lake. 'How old are you, Khadra?' the teacher asks. 'How are you liking Donegal so far?'

Mum's hand presses firm on your back. With the other hand she rocks Hamza's buggy. 'Sorry, teacher. Khadra, she speak English very good.'

'Come on, Khadra,' Mum hisses in Arabic. 'What's the problem? Tell the teacher you're eleven.' Mum's pretty eyes are angry above her blue niqab. 'Sorry,' Mum says to the teacher. 'Khadra, she little shy. Sorry.'

'No worries,' Miss Murphy smiles, and she keeps filling you up with questions. 'What's your favourite colour, Khadra? Is this your little brother here?' Other kids come tumbling into the classroom then, and Mum manoeuvres Hamza's buggy out the door. She waves goodbye to you, and makes speaking movements with her hand, fingers in a Donald Duck beak shape. Miss Murphy leaves you at the back of the class, throwing you occasional smiles of panic.

'Look, it's a new girl.' Other kids stare at you. 'How come she's got that thing on her head?' 'What's your name?' 'Where d'ya come from?' 'Teacher, how come she's not saying nothing?' From above the clock, a lady in a blue hijab is staring at you. One of her eyes is slightly skewed, and she has a circle of light around her head. Two dazed-looking orange fish are staring at you from their mossy tank on a bookshelf, and above the teacher's desk a picture of a man with a beard is also staring at you, and his heart is exploding in his chest.

At break time, you try to get as far away from everyone else as possible. Wind whispers above you in the fat green trees, and the mountains in the distance are the colour of the desert sky just before night. Where you come from the land is hard and dusty, but here everything is alive. Spongy moss coats the corners of the yard, and grass pushes through the brickwork. Beyond the school fence you can see the waterfront, lined with bright houses the colours of the hijabs the women wore in Mogadishu: pink, sun yellow, royal blue. You imagine the houses as a row of women linking arms, staring resolutely across the dark water.

The hoots of two swans flying low over the lake make you jump. Diamond shapes dig into your back from the wire fence. Skipping ropes slap the hard grey earth. 'Four, three, two, one ...'. 'Teacher, he pushed me!' 'Race you to the wall!' 'Race you back again!' In Dadaab, you used to play games like this with Aniya, and because she was smaller you would always let her win. The red dirt used to stick to your feet, and when you got back to the tent you'd draw on the white plastic sheet with your toes.

It feels scary to be alone when you're used to being in a tent with so many other kids.

'Hey.' A girl with long black braids throws herself against the fence beside you. 'I'm Saoirse. Miss Murphy says I've to mind you, so I have. How's the form?' The girl's belly is like the sandbags on the streets of Mogadishu. She smells like dead flowers. 'Speak English?' she asks slowly. 'Yeah? Moody Murphy wouldn't have made me look after ya, only I'm in trouble for calling Megan a fat slut.' She bounces against the fence and it rattles. 'And she deserved it an' all.'

It's sweaty and tight under your hijab, even though the cold is like needles in your face. You need to do something to get this girl to stay, so you kneel and lift a small white stone from beside the fence. She crouches beside you, watches you scratch-scratch-scratch on the grey earth. She laughs. 'Cool, Mickey Mouse? That's deadly, so it is. Wish I could draw like that. My mam says I can't draw for shit. You know what I was thinking, Khadra? Your name sounds like the Irish word for dog: *mádra*. That's gas isn't it, ye being from Somalia and all?'

You nod, smiling, and she laughs again, her eyes blue and glowy. The wind catches your hijab and tosses wisps of Saoirse's black hair across her face. You want her to stay close to you like this, and also you want her to disappear into a puff of smoke, like Aladdin's genie in that movie they showed that night in Dadaab. All you kids were sitting in the red dust looking up at the screen, and the white tents stood out against the big black sky.

'Geez, Khadra,' Saoirse says, 'you're wild quiet aren't you?'

'Khadra,' Dad says, 'what's this no-talking nonsense?' He's zipping up backpacks with the white hotel light polishing his bald head. 'The Home–School Liaison Officer phoned today, asking if you speak any English. I told her you've been learning English since you were four. You're probably more fluent in English than *she* is. So why are you not talking at school, Khadra? Hmm?' Rain rattles on the roof while Dad is talking, like Eebe drumming his fingers on the top of the sky. Eebe brings the rains from heaven, the *barwaaqo*, but in Ireland Eebe must be happy-happy always because he throws those rains down almost every single day.

On the dark window, you see your small face framed by your wavy hair. Behind you, the hills of Donegal are netted with the orange lights of Bunmaglinty. Dad sighs. 'Tomorrow I want to hear that you're talking in school. Understand, Khadra?' You nod and whisper, 'okay,' but your voice sounds as if it belongs to someone else. Too loud, too clear. A braver girl's voice. Hamza toddles into the bedroom. 'Look, Dad, I'm Spider-Man!'

Mum and Dad got happy again after Hamza was born. In the hospital tent in Dadaab, they passed you this screaming thing and said, '*Barakallah*, Khadra, you have a little brother.'

127

Mum thinks that Hamza has Aniya's spirit, but you know he hasn't because he's always screaming and clinging onto Mum, and Aniya never did that. About a year after Hamza started to walk, Dad said he was bringing the family to a safe place called EuRope. And you shrieked and kicked and said, 'How are we going to find Aniya if we don't stay here?'

When you return from school a few days later, Mum says, 'Come on, Khadra, let's go find our new home.' Downstairs, other Somali families are gathered in the lobby. People squeeze your cheeks and hug your mum. '*Bit-tawfiq*,' they say, '*tosbeheena 'ala khair*.' Then an old Irish man with red cheeks walks up to your dad. 'The Mohammed family, is it? I'm Jim. I've to bring yous over to the island.'

You all follow the man to his truck and climb into the front seat, with Hamza on Mum's knee. 'Fine evening, so it is.' The man whistles a tune as he drives away from the town. Sunlight filters through a bank of thin young trees, causing shadows to blink and flicker across the car windows.

'Sorry,' Dad is asking the man, 'our home, how we will reach? My daughter, she must go to school in Bunmaglinty. How we can reach? We don't have boat.'

'Ach no,' the man laughs. 'Inch Island has a causeway, so it has. A sorta bridge, like. So yous can come and go as yous please. There's a bus every hour, so I believe.'

He stops the car outside a milk-white house with yellow algae on the roof. To you, it looks as if someone has spilled turmeric all over the crooked grey tiles. You hold Dad's hand as you follow the man inside. 'It's a grand spot altogether,' the old man says, slapping dust off one of the faded lilac sofas. The musty air is heavy from not having been breathed for so long, and eyes of strange prophets watch you from the walls. You spot the man with the exploding heart who is also on your classroom wall, and you tug Mum's sleeve. 'Not now, Khadra,' she whispers.

'Aye, it's a grand spot,' the old man says. 'Outside, turn left and it'll take you down to the lake. Colony of swans down there. Hundreds of them. They come back here every year. Homing instinct, I suppose. You like feeding the swans, do you, missy?' The old man pets your head. Then he and Dad go into the kitchen, and you hear them talking about gas and electrics and the immersion switch.

You like the pictures of the strange prophets, which decorate every room and make you feel less alone in the bedroom with the sloping rafters. But after the old man has gone, Dad takes the pictures down, carefully wraps them in old towels and slides them behind the sofa.

Anseo means *here*.

Sam? *Anseo.*

Siobhán? *Anseo.*

Mark? *Anseo.*

Khadra?

You know the word to say. *Anseo.* An-sho. You've heard the other kids say it. But the word swells in your throat, and all the other kids turn to stare at you.

'*ANSEO!*' A voice calls out behind you. Saoirse is twirling the end of her braid around a biro. 'Yeah, Miss, she's here so she is.'

'Thank you, Saoirse,' Miss Murphy sighs. 'If we could just answer our *own* names please, not other people's ...'.

This morning, while the class are doing Religion, Miss Murphy brings you over to the corner of the classroom signposted OUR LIBRARY. Two bookcases lean against each other with no books on them. All the books are on the floor, flat or propped open like tents. 'I've a wee job for you,

Khadra, so I have,' Miss Murphy says. 'If you'd like to help tidy it? Do you like books?' Again she gives you that smile of panic, but you understand what she wants you to do. You sit on a damp beanbag and arrange the books with their spines the right way. Fiction books together. Non-fiction books together. *Harry Potter. Irish Rivers. Horrid Henry. Tír na nÓg.*

While you're tidying, you listen to the class learning about their God, who's called Geezus and who died on a cross-shaped piece of wood to save everyone. So how come he didn't save Aniya, and all those other people in Dadaab too? Maybe this Geezus has got confused and now he only saves *some* people. Maybe Miss Murphy should explain that a bit better so that everyone could understand. If you were teacher, you would explain everything very well and everyone would listen.

At break time, birds with torn black wings circle the yard like Huur the dreaded one bringing sad messages. You're watching the birds when Saoirse comes over and touches the side of your hijab, where no one at school is allowed to see. 'Can I ask ye, Khadra, do you ever take this yoke off?' You swallow hard. Rainclouds are gathering above the hills. Two small girls skip past with their legs and even their knees showing. My God! Don't they know Allāh is watching? And *Nadaar* the righteous one is always peeping down, looking for people who are doing something wrong, and then he'll send lightning bolts to shoot them dead. *Nidar Ba Ku Heli*, your Ayeeyo used to tell you when she caught you stealing plantains from her kitchen.

You kneel and scratch with the white stone. You draw Nadaar shooting lightning bolts out of his eyes. Saoirse laughs, 'That's class. Will you do one of them on me copybook?' She links her arm with yours.

After break, Miss Murphy sends the boys away into another room, and then she puts some pictures on the board. 'At a certain time in her life, a woman's body starts changing,' she says. 'Any idea how a woman's body changes?' In the pictures, the bits inside a woman are like a pomegranate flower. The male bits are ugly and the female bits are happier when the male bits are not there. You remember Queen Caraweelo, and how she went around chopping the male parts off all the men in her kingdom, and how Aniya and you giggled when your Ayeeyo first told you that story.

'You laughing, Khadra?' Saoirse is beside you. 'Don't get me started. You thinking about *sex*, is it?' Dimples bracket her lips, and the laughter bubbles up in you. A sudden release of wordless sound. Something between choking and crying. As if the sound is being made by a creature trapped inside you. Feathered and winged. Flexing and fluttering. Beating against your chest. Laughter hurts your belly and stings your eyes.

'Saoirse and Khadra!' Miss Murphy shouts. 'Stop laughing this instant. My goodness, girls. Khadra, I'm shocked. Of all the girls to misbehave. If you two are not mature enough to participate, you may leave the classroom. Carrying on like that ... ridiculous.'

'Come on.' Saoirse takes your arm. Next thing you're outside in the corridor, holding each other up. You trip into the cloakroom and sit in between the hung-up coats. It smells like damp feet, and your giggles simmer into hiccups. Laughter is far, far better when you're not supposed to do it. Saoirse wipes her eyes on the back of her sleeve. 'Oh my God, I've never laughed so much. You'll be my best pal, won't you, Khadra?'

'Twice!' Dad shouts, 'Twice! Two phone calls in one week. You have to help me out here, Khadra, because I just don't understand. First this school is telling me you don't speak. Next they're phoning to say that you and another girl were being disruptive in class. What's going on with you, child? *Astaghfirullah*, Khadra. You must ask Allāh for forgiveness.'

You pray together with Dad then, kneeling on the sticky lino by the kitchen window. Nearby, Hamza is making aeroplane noises from his high chair. Mum is frying beans and listening to a talk show on the radio. May Allāh azzwajal increase me in my strength and purity, you pray. But when you close your eyes, you see Saoirse's gap-toothed smile and you feel Aniya's hand in yours. You see the eyes of all those prophets following you across the room, and you see a giant swan swooping to lift the bright houses of Bunmaglinty in its beak. You open your eyes, breathing fast. Maybe your Allāh is like their Geezus. He's got confused too.

Dad hugs your shoulders. 'Promise me you'll talk in school, *habibi*? Hmm?'

You still haven't got used to the salty, fishy smell that wafts in the door when Mum opens it to bring you to school each morning. In Mogadishu the sea was an almost-constant blue that lapped and sang and crashed on sand so white it was blinding. But the sea in Donegal is alive and feral. Sometimes the lake stretches in swathes of teal and ultramarine. Other times the water darkens to the colour of the strange blocks of earth you've seen people cutting above on the hills. At these times, water swills and dumps the beach with noxious green seaweed, shells and driftwood. Waves rattle the cage of the harbour railings and hurl themselves against the rocks, but the swans don't seem to mind.

Below your house with its strange prophets and tumeric-stained roof, the lake is blotted white with hundreds of swans, which have so far resisted all of your attempts to feed them.

One day you and Hamza walk over twigs and snapping sand-coloured grasses to where two swans are sitting on the gravelly beach. The landscape is muted, pale with rain, and the lake carries sky-grey ripples that move at the speed of the clouds. Watching the water makes you feel dizzy, remembering the suck-clap of the water against the tiny boat that brought you to EuRope. That night was so dark that you could hardly see the water, and you imagine it was thicker than the water of the lake; it was more like oil or blood.

You approach the swans holding Hamza's chubby fist in one hand, a bag of week-old Brennan's bread crusts in the other. 'Bird!' Hamza laughs and points. One of the swans tucks her head under a wind-fluttered wing, and the other reaches out its beak. You reach out your hand. You can see the murky lake water reflected in the swan's black eyes. Beside you on the beach, an orange box says A STOLEN BUOY = A STOLEN LIFE.

There's a hiss and a snap. Arched wings. Razor teeth. Wings beating, scattering feathers. Your heart is doing cartwheels as you and Hamza stumble back up the lane to the house. Mum comes running and hugs you both to her skirts. There's a perforated swan-bite on your right hand, and for some reason only known to little brothers, Hamza is the one who is crying.

Days pass. The leaves on the fat green trees turn yellow and then red. Colours nibble through the branches like quick-catching fire. And the silence seeps into your skin, until it becomes bone-deep.

Life dividing into lives, already it feels as if your life in Somalia happened to somebody else. By the time the first frost hardens the lawns of Bunmaglinty, you have stopped speaking at home also. You don't say *sabāhul khayr* in the morning, or *tusbih 'alā khayr* at night. A stone of quiet hardens in your chest, somewhere beneath your ribcage. Silence cloaks you like the cape of the nomadic prophet Nebi Khadar, whom your Ayeeyo used to tell you about. 'He wanders the streets between sunset and night disguised as a beggar,' she'd say. 'You'll know him by his strange handshake, for he has a thumb without any bone in it.' This story used to scare you, the thought of that creepy handshake, but now you see yourself as Nebi Khadar, covered in the invisibility cloak of your quiet.

You hear things you shouldn't. Being silent makes people think you're deaf, and they say whatever they want in your vicinity. 'There's this new girl in our class who doesn't speak,' one boy tells another in the yard. Beside you in class, two girls trade secrets without bothering to whisper. 'So he says that she says that he fancies you, so he does.' Miss Murphy dies her hair black and stops giving you smiles of panic. Instead, she writes 'Excellent' on the bottom of your homework. 'Lovely work, Khadra. If only the rest of the class were so well behaved. Beautiful handwriting.'

One morning, a strange woman takes you out of class to the PE hall. 'Breathe in deeply,' the strange woman says. 'Fill your lungs, and now … releeeease the sooouuund, hmmmmmmmm.' This woman has very long ears like Dhegdheer. Maybe she goes around eating lost children, and what will you do if she tries to eat you? 'Copy the shapes of my lips, Khadra,' the woman says. 'I'm going to help you to speak.' This PE hall has too much space inside it, not enough corners in which to hide. 'Breathe in,' the woman says, 'breathe out … breathe in …'.

You open your lips, but all that emerges is emptiness, dark as the desert you crossed.

The Dhegdheer woman frowns. 'Perhaps that will be enough for today,' she says. When she takes you back to class, the stares of the other kids trip you up. 'Depending on the level of trauma, it can be quite a long process,' that strange woman tells Miss Murphy. But she doesn't know about the noise your mum let out of her when she saw that Aniya was gone.

'Well, she *was* in a refugee camp,' Miss Murphy whispers close.

'Gosh,' the strange woman says, 'really?'

'Hmm,' Miss Murphy says, but the class are noisy, so all you can hear is 'Dadaab' and 'Mediterranean' and then 'Christ God Love Her The Poor Wee Thing.' Both women's faces go red as if they're going to cry, and they look down at you with watery-eyed smiles.

In the yard, Saoirse puts a kiss on your cheek. The yard is dusted white, and your fingers tingle with cold. Saoirse's lips are damp moth wings, and you'd like to wipe the kiss away. 'Will you be on our team for the debates, Khadra? You know what a debate is, right?' You nod. Miss Murphy has been talking about the Bunmaglinty Debating Championships all week. Proposing and Opposing. Ireland should offer to rehome more refugees. For and Against. 'We need an extra person,' Saoirse says. 'You'll help us, will you?'

She looks at you as if you're meant to do something. But you don't know what to do. You shake your head, and you feel Saoirse's anger steaming on you then. 'What do you mean, "no"? Why not? After I've been friends with you and all, why wouldn't you give us a wee bit of help? Miss Murphy says you *can* talk. So why won't you say something, Khadra? Just one *word*. Will you just *whisper* something to me?'

Saoirse leans with her head so close you can smell the grease of her hair. Words bubble in your throat. If you made one sound, you might say everything. From the trapdoor of your lips, machine-gun fire would pour. You would speak about the smell of the tarpaulin on the lorry where you hid, the first sight of white tents stretching to the horizon, the stench of Dadaab in your hair, Aniya's clammy hand in yours, that listless, always-alert kind of sleep in a port town rumbling with trucks, and the way the small boat swayed beneath your feet. If you said something, you might not stop. From your lips it might all spill out and flood the yard. Saoirse steps back. Her mouth is a firm line. 'Forget it,' she says. 'You don't wanna talk to me, and you don't wanna be on our team. You're useless, so you are. Useless as *fuck*.'

As Saoirse runs away from you, those birds caw-caw-caw again, making your tummy jump. 'I tagged you!' 'No you didn't!' 'Yes I did!' 'TEACHER! Those kids are trying to get onto our imaginary bus!'

The universe balances itself on the horns of a bull, your Ayeeyo told you. And now you can see that brown bull balancing rain and sun and stars above its head until it gets dizzy and everything spins and falls into the wrong place. There's no sun in this sky. If you stay very still, perhaps you will disappear into their cotton-wool clouds. Across the yard, Saoirse is talking and laughing with those other girls. A white-haired girl's skinny arm is wrapped in the canyons of Saoirse's belly folds. When those girls look at you, they laugh.

For the rest of the day, you don't even think about Aniya or Dadaab or the boat on the dark-dark sea. Saoirse sits in front of you with her long ponytail sliding like a scorpion tail down her back, so close you could touch it. You see the small hairs on Saoirse's neck. You see the backs of her pink earlobes. When it's PE, you pretend to Miss Murphy that you're sick, and she lets you stay in the classroom to tidy

The Library. *Cinderella. National Geographic. Where's Wally? Amazing Facts About Egypt.* This time you arrange those broken books: fiction, non-fiction, fiction, non-fiction.

Outside the window, the lake is a gash of black between white-dusted mountains, and bare sycamores wear green balaclavas of ivy. Nests are clots of dark in the dead branches. The other kids tumble back into the room, red-faced and sweaty, hanging up their PE kits, talking about snow.

'She's a *mute*,' you hear Saoirse snigger to a girl beside her. And just before lunch break you take a pair of classroom scissors and hide them up your sleeve.

Hot up your sleeves, the scissors slip. Why won't Saoirse come to you? For twenty minutes you've watched her laughing with those other girls, and now the yard bell trills.

First bell means FREEZE. All those kids are like statues. Imagine if everyone in Dadaab had stood still like that and you had skipped through them, finding Aniya. Mum says Aniya's *ayaanie* now, which means she's an angel. But one day you'll go back to Somalia, and then you'll search and find her.

Second bell means walk to your line, NO RUNNING. All the kids are walking to their lines, but one person is running across the yard with a pink fur-lined coat and a sandbag belly. Saoirse squeezes into the line in front of you. She throws a glance at you and then whispers something to the girl in front of her. Little biting words pinch you, like *kaneecos* sipping your blood in the night-time in Dadaab.

'Who's that talking?' Everyone shuts up while the teacher chooses the best class line. It's so quiet that you can even hear the wind fluttering the Irish flag on the roof. Caw-caw-caw, those black birds are still wheeling around the sky, like they're trying to find something they've lost. Burning in your palm, the classroom scissors melt into your fingers. You imagine reaching out to snap them on Saoirse's ponytail, the clod of hair thumping to your feet like a dead rat and Saoirse spinning around with her hacked hair whipping across her face. You imagine the shock in Saoirse's eyes. A shock that would tell you she *knows*. She sees you. And you see her too.

It's loud in your head, like when that gunshot sounded in Dadaab and you saw all those people scattering and Aniya's hand leaving yours. It feels as if your heart might explode like that strange prophet's, sending beams of light shooting across the yard. 'HALF A MILLION PEOPLE!' the man in Dadaab with the shiny gold badge shouted at your mum. 'HOW do you expect us to find one child, missus? *HOW?*'

The bell ripples across the yard, and the silence is gone.

Lines of children start snaking inside, two by two. Saoirse walks in front of you with her ponytail swinging. At the door, she turns and looks back. She gives you a small smile, almost too small to see, and your belly melts. Maybe tomorrow Saoirse will be your Best Pal again and you'll whisper secret things. You'll tell her how you cried when Mum said you were leaving Dadaab to try to get to EuRope. How the small boat chug-chug-chugged and then stopped. And how L-A-M-P-E-D-U-S-A was just a few small lights on the back of the churning sea. You'll tell her about the silver blanket they wrapped you in, and the cold place with boxes and flowers on their lids. You'll tell her about landing in Ireland and thinking the whole world had frozen. And you'll tell her about Aniya.

Tonight, you will pray to Allāh Who is Truly the Most Just to find your sister and bring her here to you. Just before you go to sleep, you'll untie your braid, and your hair will wave against your skin, as wild and as quiet as water.

When Time Stretches

Puddles of sky map the Dublin runway as the plane lifts into the blue. As we break through the clouds, the Fasten Seatbelt sign pings off and I turn on my iPod, scrolling through playlists in search of something tranquil. *Clair de Lune* seems like a safe choice. Music floods through my headphones, and I wrap the headphone wire around my finger as I rehearse the journey in my head. Dublin to Dubai, a two-hour layover, then Dubai to Yogyakarta, where you are.

'It's a business trip,' I lied to my ex-wife on the phone last night. At first I'd intended not to tell her I was going anywhere at all. But then I imagined car wrecks, twisted metal and my landline ringing into the silence of my apartment. 'It's a conference on network communication in Kuala Lumpur,' I lied. 'Matt from the office was meant to go, but he's come down with the flu, so they're sending me.'

'God, Alex. That must have cost a fortune,' Debbie said, 'a last-minute ticket like that.'

'Mad money,' I agreed, remembering the €2,400 I'd charged to my card.

'Still, it's the company's money, I suppose.'

'I just do as I'm told.'

'It'll be good for you to get a break away, love.'

The ease with which Debbie accepted my lie made me feel worse about it.

I lean back against the headrest, closing my eyes. I couldn't tell Debbie I was going to Yogyakarta. She'd only have worried. And she'd have asked questions I couldn't have answered. My need to reach you only makes sense in my head. Perhaps if I were to express it, my logic would dissolve. Already I can sense your anxiety. Don't worry, Iman. My telling of our story can't hurt you now, across this time, this distance. Trust me: there will be no more shards of pain. Now it's just my words, spoken in broken Javanese, carried on my tongue by pure muscle memory.

'Out of his head,' Batari whispered on the phone the other night. Your mother's fluty voice was almost as I'd last heard it twenty years ago, but scratched by the gravel of tears. She paused only briefly to explain how she'd found my number on my company's website, with the help of your brother, Ande, before cutting straight to her plea: 'Please come quick to Yoyga, mister Alex, or Iman he'll be gone.'

At her words, a jigsaw piece slotted into place. So that was why I've been seeing your smile in cloud shapes lately. And why, at nights, I've often shuddered awake in reasonless panic. I know you're hurting. You know I know. I can sense your pain from across the planet. Others might think it odd, Iman, but stranger things happen every day. We've always been soul-twins, you and I. My only question is, how much do you remember about the night of the shadow-puppet play? And how much do you want to forget?

Growing up in Yogyakarta, I recall soft rain, the fragrance of the mango groves, and always the sound of the gamelan, chiming through my childhood. I used to imagine that the *bonangs* and *kempuls* were pots with the music cooking inside them. An ensemble of percussion instruments, tuned gongs and hand drums, the gamelan is Indonesia's most time-honoured musical tradition. It was the gamelan that brought me to you. Or to be exact, it was my father's PhD on 'Aural Transmission for Karawitan', which had brought my parents from Dublin to the sultanate of Yogyakarta in 1986 when I was three. My dad's gamelan compositions, developed during his studies at South Bank University, had caught the attention of Sultan Yamenbulowanyo the Twelfth on his visit to London in '83. Eager to forge ties with Western musicians, the sultan had appointed my father as Musical Director of his palace gamelan. Not only that, but he had invited my parents to come and live in the artists' quarter of his palace in Yogyakarta, where your dad was the *kuncen* – caretaker.

We were the only Irish family living in the palace compound, where white-washed houses with colonial-style porches and wooden fronts resembled the set of an old western. You'd almost have expected to meet Roy Rogers and Trigger trotting down one of the red-dirt streets. Adding to the mismatched feel of the place were gas lamps, complete with fleur-de-lis columns, which might have surfaced from the Narnia books you and I loved. The grid of streets centred on the *kraton*, residence of the sultan and his extended family. Built in a similar pistols-at-dawn style to the houses that surrounded it, the *kraton* was an odd place, a jumble of snake-patterned pillars, palm groves, tiled courtyards and ceremonial pagodas.

To the west of the *kraton* stood two shaggy banyans fenced by intricate white railings. The twin banyans had roots in the Dutch colonial era, I'd been told, when

Indonesia was referred to as the 'emerald necklace of the Pacific.' Myth had it that a Javanese princess was engaged to be married to a man she disliked intensely. Eager to get out of the engagement, she set him a challenge that if he could pass between the twin banyans he would have her hand. Each time the man tried to walk between the trees, he was felled by an invisible power surge between the trunks, and so the princess was free. There were those who said the left tree was a gateway to the Southern Sea; that closing your eyes and walking straight between the trees would purify a person's heart and grant their deepest wishes. It was one of many places in Yogya that made me uneasy; to walk between the banyans was to experience a sense of being watched.

Fear was never far away in the royal sultanate. One of my earliest memories of Yogya is of my father bringing me to Pak Mulwono's workshop on Jalan Sedewa to watch a new gamelan being built. Molten metal sent a fierce red glow up the walls of the cavern, stacked high with metal instruments in various stages of completion. I stepped closer to a glowing *kempul*, mesmerised by the heat. Pak Mulwono roared something at me in Indonesian, and my dad grabbed my hand and pulled me away from the furnace. 'Jesus Christ, Alexander! Didn't I tell you it was dangerous? Didn't I?'

He slapped the back of my hand, and I cried the whole way home to the *kraton*, around all the winding red-dirt streets, back to the artists' quarter. I was still crying when my dad went out to his evening rehearsal with the palace musicians. My tears had slowed to rasping hiccups, when there was a rap at our door.

Mam opened the groaning wooden shutter, letting in the chirping humidity of the Javanese night. A small Indonesian woman stood on our porch step, with an infant of about my age clinging to the fuchsia folds of her sari. 'Batari,' she pressed a hand to her chest, 'Iman,' she indicated you. The porch light drew blue zigzags in your mama's black hair and caught the red dot of her bindi. She held up a tub of mango lassi, 'For your little boy, he crying, yes?'

'Come in, come in.' My mam took the tub of oozing yellow lassi and ushered your mama into our narrow wooden kitchen. Batari, it turned out, spoke good English, and worked part-time as a tour guide for Yogakarta Exciting Visits. Green tea was poured, a savoured packet of Mikado biscuits opened, and the kettle put to boil yet again. Relaying the story of how she had ended up in Yogyakarta against her wishes, my mam sobbed in your mother, Batari's, arms, while you and I eyed each other between table legs with the fearless curiosity of infants. Tears dried sticky on my face, my tantrum quickly forgotten.

Iman, did you ever think it strange that we lived in the grounds of a palace? It's weird how realities experienced in childhood can seem universal. I never imagined any reality other than Yogya, just like I could never have imagined a day without you in it.

My father's initial placement in Java was to last for ten months, but this stretched into two years. Then three. Then four. The stall owners stopped charging my mother tourist prices in Pasar Beringharjo, where she haggled over pungent meats, leafy spinach or bright red chilli peppers. Our small wooden house became cluttered with Irish paraphernalia posted by Dublin relatives. And I started Tumbah Primary School, where I sat at a rickety-lidded desk, took part in volcano drills, and learnt to read Javanese from the *Ramayana*.

'But what about Alex?' I heard my mother whisper on the porch one night, 'What about his education, Henry? This isn't fair.'

'Christ, Laura,' my father's voice was sharp. 'If I've told you once.... My mother is more than willing for Alex to go and live with her in Greystones.'

'On the other side of the world!' My mother's voice trembled as if it might break. 'How could you send your son to the other side of the world, Henry!'

'You could go with him,' he replied. In my mother's silence, the porch swing squealed. I imagined my father standing abruptly. 'I always told you I didn't want children, Laura. Alexander was a mistake, and you wouldn't hear reason. We'll talk about this when you've calmed down.'

Listening breathless from behind my mosquito net, I knew my father must have been confused. Mistakes were small, forgotten things, like dropped mangoes, bruised and squishy, or a batik shirt ripped from climbing the gayam trees with you. How could something as big as a whole person be a mistake? Besides, I knew my father loved me because he had given me Sita, a *wayang-kulit* puppet, her face silver and bowed. This was the mark of her nobility, my father had explained excitedly when he'd handed her to me on my fifth birthday, wrapped in rough camel-coloured paper. 'Oh,' my mam had cooed, 'a doll?'

'It's not a doll, it's an ornament,' my father had said, 'and not to be played with. Boys don't play with dolls, do they, Alex?'

I cradled the puppet, studying the way her head was chiselled into an elaborate headdress. Glass beads rattled gently against her face. Stilts controlled her spindly silver willow arms. 'The nobility of the *Ramayana* all have bowed heads and silver faces, Alexander,' my father told me. 'You see the markings around her eyes? This symbolises the intricacies of her moral evolution in the Mencari Sita stages of the *Ramayana* …'.

As he talked, I looked at his shining bald patch and ruddy, fluttering hands. I wondered why Mam and I never made him happy like this. My father's face only took on this excited flush when he spoke about the gamelan, and his eager smile made him almost good-looking. Later that evening I watched my mam standing on the porch, smoking with her slender arms folded. Her ash-blonde hair was bright in the sway of a storm lantern, her skin pale as the inside of potato peel as she stared out into the riot of the chirruping dark.

I suppose my dad had hoped I would be a great gamelan composer like him, but I was born without a note of musicality in my body. All gamelan music sounded the same to me, no different from the twitter of caged canaries in Pasar Ngasem, or the cries of street hawkers in the winding entrails of Jalan Solo. When all attempts to teach me to play the *kempuls* had failed, at the age of eight I was relegated to the piano, at which I underperformed just as spectacularly.

The afternoon before the shadow-puppet play, I sat at the piano in our living room, surrounded by black reflections of my awkward fingers. You stuck your tongue out at me through the tall sash windows, and my arthritic piano teacher, Bu Sukarto, insisted, 'One more time, Alexander, from the top.'

My fingers tripped over each other and struggled between notes. Time moved achingly on the mantelpiece clock. It was with relief that I watched the minute hand hiccup onto three o'clock. I slid off the cracked leather piano stool and grabbed my rucksack. 'Don't forget to practice,

Alexander!' Bu Sukarto called as I skipped out of the house, into the hot lion's-breath air of the porch.

'Come on, slowcoach,' you teased, 'I've been waiting for *decades*.'

'Cowabunga!' We chased each other between the laughing fountains, through sunlight so high that you could stand in your own shadow.

Panting and content, we collapsed onto a pagoda. From there we watched your father sweep the flagstones, cool in his loose white tunic. My dad paced after him, his bald patch pink with sunburn, veins in his neck throbbing like sitar strings tuned too tightly. It was like watching one of the graceful palace elephants being annoyed by an angry mosquito. 'Jesus Christ, where are the new *kempuls*?' my father squawked at yours. 'Honest to God, Susilo! Why haven't you prepared the instruments for tonight's *wayang-kulit*?'

'*Jam karet*,' your father shrugged. *Time stretches.*

We giggled as the two men disappeared behind one of the pagodas. You rolled over, bringing your nose close to mine, and I tried to find the pupil in your inky eyes. 'Next game, hide-and-seek,' you announced. 'GO, Alex-ji. I'll count from ten.' You bowed your head over your skinny arms, and I noticed the comma of white skin on your crown, where your thick black hair tufted up in unruly spikes. 'Ten … nine … eight … seven …'.

'Wait, Iman, wait! You're counting too fast!'

'Am not!'

'No fair! Start over, Iman!'

'Ten … nine …'.

You were always better at hiding than I was, able to blend in against the tiny cabin where your family lived, or to crawl under the porch of my family's house, your black hair camouflaged by the shadows. I could never hide from you for long, always betrayed by my gingery hair protruding from behind a mossy fountain, or a pale arm glimpsed trembling with laughter in the almond shade.

'Six … five …'.

I scarpered behind a flowering buddleia bush by the artificial lake, and cowered down, tucking my knees to my chest. In the lake, gold and scarlet fish lurked under the gaze of imported black swans. Thousand-eyed empire butterflies flitted between cones of wilting purple buddleia. I was peeking out for you between the flowers when a yellow dress flickered through the mango grove nearby, and my mother's crimped hair was caught in the discs of sunlight. Behind her, I recognised Prince Guntur, the sultan's eldest son, whose smooth BBC accent always made me suspect there was a puppet master speaking behind him, like a hidden *dalang*. The prince stroked my mother's cheek, and her bright figure was swallowed by the dark shoulders of his jacket.

'Found you!' You pounced on me with a giddy milk-toothed smile. Wrestling away from you, I looked back to the treeline, but my mother and the prince had gone. It had been a moment as fleeting as a willow leaf spinning onto the artificial lake. Small and yet significant, in the way one falling leaf can signal a change of season.

'Come on, slowcoach.' You grabbed my sleeve. 'Let's go find something to eat. *Apakah kamu lapar?*'

'Starving,' I replied.

We raced each other out of the palace compound to the dusty roadside markets along Jalan Suryowijayan. With a sweaty fistful of my pocket money, we bought a *masala dosa* from Mr Roy's New Delhi stall. Then we ran into the delicious gloom of Taman Sari, the ruined pleasure garden. As we lazed amidst stars of wild narcissi, your fingers started at one end of the *masala dosa*, mine at the other. Talking with our mouths full, we tore off handfuls from each end of the roll until our greasy fingers squabbled over the remainders of yellow rice in the centre.

Appetites sated, we played rounds of Connect Four, tried to get my rusty Slinky to bounce down the steps of a fountain, and took turns at swinging each other in our white muslin hammock; an old bed sheet of my mother's that we had strung up between two banyans for this purpose. A low coo of fruit pigeons echoed from the branches, accompanied by the racket of piping crows and the symphony of insects. A thread of smoke meandered across the skyline from the rim of the Gunung Merapi, as if the mountain were brooding over its next eruption. You followed my frown to the smoking horizon and laughed, 'Not to worry, Alexander-ji slowcoach. The sultan sahib controls the mountain and keeps *all* people safe.'

I didn't believe you. Yamenbulowanyo the Twelfth was a short, bald man with tiny slippered feet and a permanent worry line between his brows. He didn't seem like any match for the towering blue silhouette of the active volcano. Nor for the clouds above the *kraton*, which seemed about to break. I remembered Prince Guntur's hand on my mother's arm. Her bright hair swallowed by his shoulders. The angry veins in my father's neck. And perhaps it was to ease my frown that you said, 'I have it, a plan for tonight after the *wayang-kulit*. The best, best plan. Are you ready, mister Alex-ji? Hmm?'

Iman. I'm travelling to reach you at forty-thousand feet, across darkness broken only occasionally by the lights of desert towns, splattered on the black in strange patterns, like unknown zodiac signs. You can think what I tell you a confession if you like, but one woven from half-remembered fragments. Memories, which may or may not be real. It's as if we've been hiding from each other for almost twenty years. Eyes covered, counting backwards from a hundred until we meet again.

People don't *do* this, do they? They don't hold on to the memory of childhood friends like this. I can imagine the ridicule I'd meet if I confided this story to anyone in the office, or any of my friends. But some people's childhood friendships are different. Some people's fates are intertwined. I've never forgotten you, Iman, and I've never forgotten that night.

What if I'm too late? The thought has crossed my mind. Your calm mother, Batari, was always a person to under-exaggerate a calamity. My only hope is to keep on travelling and telling this story to you, praying you might hear me. So, I continue on my pilgrimage, drawn as if by the tug of the moon. I trundle through another glassy airport, where desert winds quarrel with the windows. And onwards through security checks and passport control, my wheelie-bag bumping up escalators, down plastic tunnels and around corners, over the metal lip, onto another plane. Iman, I will lay my memories at your feet like gifts of the lost Magi from across the continents. I must only reach you and whisper our story to you, and then you'll be okay.

Your plan was simple. After the shadow-puppet play, we would sneak back to Taman Sari and sleep outside in the hammock. 'An all-night adventure, Alexander-ji,' you grinned, 'Connect Four till dawn! Plus all the grown-ups will be dozing at the *wayang-kulit*, so no one will know. What do you say?'

All through the performance, I perched by my mother's side and watched palace musicians in black silk shirts and batik belts sit cross-legged at the brass pot-like instruments. Shadows of Rama and Sita emerged on the translucent screen, illuminated by the soft light of the coconut-husk lamp. Out of sight, the *dalang* manipulated the puppets' spindly willow-arms to indicate which character was speaking, weaving tales from the *Ramayana* deep into the night. As the *sindhen* kept up their wailing song, my father played the bamboo flute, his shoulders held back proudly. Shivering candles turned his glasses into bright squares of light, hiding his eyes.

'Mam,' I whispered, 'are you bored too?'

'Shhh, *a stór*,' she smiled. Her filigree earrings sent meteorites across the parquet flooring. I laid my head on the lap of her silky evening dress, and from this angle watched Prince Guntur pretending not to look in our direction.

The wedding scene marked midnight as always, and at the vows of Sita and Rama, Mam took my hand. 'Come on, Alexander, time for bed.'

No sooner had she tucked me into bed and shut my bedroom door, than the first of your pebbles hit my shutter and I scrambled from the mosquito net. Below the porch, you smiled up at me, 'Come on, slowcoach.'

Heart galloping, I stepped into my slippers and skidded out onto the porch. I ran towards our meeting-place, beside the twin banyans, massive in the darkness. The red-dirt streets were deserted as we ran from there through the maze of the *kraton*. From the main palace building came the chiming of the gamelan song *'Udan Mas'*, which I knew meant 'Golden Rain'. Doleful at first, the music became more frantic the faster we ran. Chiming notes chased us across the palace compound, until we reached the luxurious dark of Taman Sari. Serious now, we hung our bedsheet between the trees, shivering in a night air sweet with Arabian jasmine.

Iman. Sleeping in the hammock between the banyans with you was nicer than sleeping alone on the hard mattress of my creaking cot. But the hypnotic, swimming dances of the shadow-puppets had got into our heads. So, rather than playing Connect Four for hours as we'd intended, we soon fell asleep in the hammock's folds. Your breath smelt of mango lassi, and the oblong of muslin squished us together like twins in an embryonic sack. Our heartbeats fell into sync.

Sometime after midnight, I woke to a humid night loud with chirruping crickets, singing tree-frogs and the scratch of cicadas. You were snoring beside me, soft-limbed with sleep, your long lashes like dark commas on your cheeks. I peered out across the clearing. At first I thought my mother was being suffocated under Prince Guntur's weight, then he pulled back and their figures separated. Mam bowed her head, pale-faced in the moonlight, a length of white muslin gathered around her shoulders. As the prince brought her hand to his lips, her arm hung limp, as if an invisible puppet-master were controlling her movements with stilts of bamboo.

I turned to find your eyes wide open, your stare fixed not on my mother and the prince, but on a figure at the edge of the clearing. Without his glasses, my father craned his neck and the moonlight made a cap on his bald patch. From where he stood he could only have seen the prince's silhouette, and he seemed to be studying the scene as if it were a crucial stanza from the *Ramayana*. Perhaps the moment when Rama and Laksamana search for Sita by a pond of lotuses, and are attacked by a crocodile. Or the moment when Rama wrestles the crocodile, kills it, and releases the spirit of a cursed angel who had been trapped in crocodile form. My father watched my mother stand on tiptoe to kiss the prince's cheek. Watched her hurry away, her movement dancing between the trees.

As my father's eyes swooped towards us, we ducked back down into the hammock. My heart was too loud for me to speak. I nestled against your shoulder, imagining we were wrapped in a chrysalis and would emerge with wings.

'Jesus Christ,' my father's voice made us both shriek. He tipped the hammock, and we fell onto the hard earth. 'What under God's name are you two doing out here?'

'Iman, run!' I shouted, and we took off across Taman Sari. Birds that had lullabied us only moments earlier now screeched and yelled. I kept on running, afraid that a thousand beaks would lunge and peck out my eyes. Our plimsolls pummelled the maze of dirt tracks back through the compound, where whitewashed buildings stood ghostly blue in the early light.

'Tomorrow, Alex-ji,' you whispered as you slipped into your cabin.

Sides aching, I ran up our porch steps, spotting the crumpled batik skirt of my puppet Sita under the porch swing. I grabbed the dusty puppet, ran to my room and dived into bed. I shut my eyes and clasped Sita to my chest. The hard skull of her face dug against my ribcage.

Is it shame that's kept me from you these twenty years, Iman? Or fear of the anger I imagined in you?

When I hung up the phone after speaking to your mother, Batari, I leaned back in my office chair and stared at my reflection on the dark office window. I suppose people would say I've done well. My docklands apartment offers a view over Grand Canal Dock from three of its four balconies. I have no wife or children, but a comfortable living. Before we broke up, Debbie often said, 'Alex, it's as if you're hiding something. You never let me get close to you.' I denied it at the time.

I have ended every relationship at the point where the past slid into view. I've never told anyone about you. I've cradled our story inside me for two decades, as if to speak it might have broken the spell.

Two nights ago, I clicked onto a flight-comparison website and typed in 'Dublin-Yogyakarta'. Even the act of clicking 'search' came as a lightning bolt of freedom. I'd been holding my breath for twenty years, and had finally exhaled.

The morning after the shadow-puppet play brought the clatter of birds on the galvanised roof. A splinter smarted in my finger from cradling the wooden puppet Sita all night. My heartbeat had quickened as if I'd been chased in my dreams. Wall panels creaked with damp, and a tiny sand-coloured gecko crawled up my bedroom wall.

At breakfast, my father buttered his toast with rough strokes. 'You're coming with me today, Alexander.'

'Where's Mam?'

'Never mind. You're comin' with me. And Iman's comin' too.'

Minutes later, we picked you up from your father's hut. You shuffled out onto the porch, Batari ruffling your hair. Your nutmeg skin was doing its best to camouflage a blue-and-yellow bruise. 'He said he fell out of bed in the night,' she laughed. 'Will you keep an eye on him?'

'I will,' my father replied.

I looked at you sideways and didn't know what to say. Memory of the previous night walked alongside us, as unsayable as a long word neither of us could read. Mutely, we followed my father out of the palace compound. Down Jalan Polowijan and Jalan Kidipaten. Across the murky River Kali Code to Pak Mulwono's workshop on Jalan Sedewa, where the sultan's new gamelan instruments were made. As we stepped into the gloom, my father muttered something about a new *kempul* and then barked at us, 'The two of you, stay put. Don't touch anything.'

The dirt floor of the workshop had been trampled into rough grey marble by the workers' feet. Sweat shone on the men's bare chests. Their trousers were turned up at the calves, and their tall shadows darted above the furnaces like frantic demons chasing Sita through the forest. Ash coated the young men's heads, as if from a funeral pyre. They worked, sweated, chewed and called out to each other above the din. I liked these men, whose open faces and honest labour was about a thousand light-years away from the batik belts and silk cushions of the sultan's nightly recitals.

I peeked from behind my father's side, and watched as the workers beat a red-hot *kempul* into shape. Their mallets hammered out a discordant tune, not unlike the gamelan music that floated into my bedroom at nights from the all-night *warang*. But this music was harsher than normal gamelan chimes. It tasted like pocket-money coins in sweaty palms. 'Dad,' I tugged his sleeve, 'have to go, Dad. Please can we go, Dad? Have to pee ...'.

Without looking at me, my father said, 'Tell me, Alexander, who was the man your mother was with last night?'

The sides of the *kempul* curved into a gong shape, and the hammering picked up tempo. My father began to dance. He clapped and swayed, pacing from foot to foot. Light from the red-hot coals leapt across his smiling face.

Workers glanced up at him, then at each other. 'Who was he, Alexander?' my father said. 'Was it Susilo?' I stared at him, wanting to run but rooted to the marbled grey earth. 'Was it Susilo, Alexander? Fuckin' answer me.'

You stepped from the shadows then, as if glimpsed in a game of hide-and-seek. I think you wanted to protect me. To say something to my dad. But the sight of your soft face, so like your father, Susilo's, sparked something in him. Without ceasing his dance, he stepped towards you and grabbed hold of your tunic. There was a moment when you and he seemed to be a single creature with many thrashing arms and legs, like the cosmic many-limbed dance of Shiva Nataraja. The reddish light blurred everything. Perhaps it happened in less than a second. My father let go, and you tripped.

'Iman blame himself,' Batari said, 'for you leave Yogya ... and for your parents separate. He think he to blame, Alexander. He think that why you don't come back. He don't want eat ... he don't want live. He will die, Alexander. You don't come, Iman he die.'

Iman. Your name means faithful. All these years, I've been presuming you blamed me. Can't you see? No one was less to blame than the child they carried from the workshop with his fingers covering his face, bright rivulets of blood trickling between his knuckles. And when the pulsing red-and-blue lights had carried you away to another place, I sat in the red dust with my wooden Sita doll in my arms, holding my elbows, shocked beyond tears. My dad brought me home in a rattling tuk-tuk, to find our mothers sitting on our porch in each other's arms. This time, both of them were crying.

Monsoon came early that year, sweeping down off the Gunung Merapi with the suddenness of a Javanese nightfall.

Banyans bowed their heads against the deluge. Air became liquid. 'We're going home,' my mam said, her voice trembling as she folded clothes into a suitcase, tucking each shirt's arms behind its back.

'Home?' I had never known a home other than Yogya. 'Is Dad coming?'

'No, *a stór*. Dad's staying here.'

'And Iman?'

She shook her head, pressed her lips together and lowered her eyes. Her blue eyelids flickered like empire butterfly wings. 'He's alive, Alex. It's just that he tripped … the furnace … Iman won't be able to see again.'

Two days later, our plane took off into bruised violet-pink clouds, which parted momentarily as the molten sun sank into the Gunung Merapi. Trails of coral-pink bled across the horizon, as if the volcano had finally spewed its contents into the sky. And the rains followed us back across the planet to Ireland, this 'home' I had only ever imagined.

As the Boeing 747 screeches onto the runway at Adisucipto, an announcement sings out, 'Welcome to Yogyakarta special district, home of the royal sultanate.'

Grass verges blaze livid green against grey asphalt. Palms toss their wet manes in the rain. Being closer to you now makes my throat tighten, my heart quicken with the impatience of years. Now that it's only a matter of minutes, I can no longer wait. 'Sir,' an air steward points to my waist, 'you cannot take off your seatbelt yet.'

I click it back. 'Sorry.'

Just breathe.

Last night, Batari's breath rattled down the phone in response to my question. Why? Why get in touch now, after all these years? Finally, she replied, 'He's turning thirty, you know.' Her words struck an instinctive logic in me, in the way that prayers in another language can be understood without translation. Yes, I know. In the weeks leading up to my thirtieth, I've seen my life flash before my eyes. All sins must be atoned for. All failures confessed. We are soul twins, you and me. It seems we even share the same paranoia.

It wasn't Prince Gumptur of course. Nor your father, Susito. Mam told me years later, during one of those awkward confessional conversations, that her lover had been a palace chauffeur, one of those men in charcoal suits, their skins the colour and texture of chamois leather, who used to wait against the black gleam of the royal Mercedes. 'It was stupid,' my mam said to me. 'He hardly spoke any English. But your dad, Alex ... I just wanted to escape.'

I nodded while she talked, and thought of you. Of the exact pattern on the shorts I was wearing on the day we left.

Things seem smaller after two decades. The airport bus pulls away to reveal the *kraton*, dull as a faded photograph. Dishevelled tourists queue for tickets to the palace grounds, mostly dressed in a mixture of gaudy raincoats and Bermuda shorts. Each seems over- or under-prepared for the monsoon. Even the sultan's gold-winged shield over the palace entrance seems like a tackier version of itself.

I hail a cab, step in and slam the door. 'You come here for holiday?' the driver asks.

'No, I came to see a friend.'

'You must see the *kraton*,' he continues. 'Number one tourist attraction. And beautiful gamelan. We have the gamelan festival here at moment. Beautiful gamelan tonight. You know the *wayang-kulit*?'

'Sure, the shadow ...'.

'*Wayang-kulit* it's mean shadow-puppet. Once in lifetime. You must to see.'

He drops me on the bridge at Jalan Sugeng Jeroni. I can walk from here. Yogyakarta is etched on my mind like the memory of a lover's skin. I know my way to your house without looking at a map. It's like dressing in the dark, even after all these years.

Palms glitter, diaphanous after the rain.

You ease the door open a fraction and step onto the porch. Batari's worried call bounces down the narrow hall behind you. Your hair, grown to your shoulders, is now threaded with white, like mine. A faded black T-shirt hangs on the wire coat hanger of your collarbone. You're thin. Too thin. There's a deathly tinge to your chapped lips and hollow cheeks. Your unseeing eyes are creased, perhaps from gazing skywards for too long. But your palms remember. Your fingers close around mine with a newborn's instinctive grip.

Iman. *Mo chara.* It's me.

Death and the Architect

I lost track of time, and she darted away from me down a dark Barcelona street. My top hat flipped off my head and my coat was a swallow's tail behind me as I ran to keep up with her. I glimpsed time's impish face smiling as she ducked behind the shoulder of a six-winged gargoyle. And thus it began.

I searched for time down every alley in the *Barri Gòtic*, where ivy leaves drip from rusty balconies, and shadows splinter in the crevices of the Gothic cathedral. I pursued time around each corner of El Raval, where ladies of the night beckoned me, stroking my beard and enquiring if they could provide a little something of what I was looking for. In their tarnished pendants I saw my own refection; a sincere Nordic face with a dandy's moustache and eyes of overly ambitious blue. Turning from those tempting lips, I struggled up the spine of La Rambla and trekked the tree-lined boulevards of the Eixample. As daylight faded, with burning bones I searched the pine-needled stillness of the *Montjuïc* forests. But time remained elusive, and I could only hear her whispering somewhere just beyond my dreams.

On impulse one night, I caught the train out to the town of Vic to seek the wisdom of my old friend Padre Josep. As I waited for my friend to finish saying the evening Mass, I studied the famous frescos of Vic Cathedral, which offer an exhaustive menu of ways in which to spend one's time in hell. The devil's face in the painting above my head had the tantalising snarl of Señor Rogent when he handed me my architect's diploma. 'We have given this academic scroll to either a madman or a genius … time will tell.' From floor to ceiling the tortured bodies of the saints writhed and twisted. San Antonio knelt with his body porcupined by arrows. Santa Lucia uncomplainingly held her own eyes on a plate.

'Good to see you, Señor Gaudí.' Padre Josep kissed my cheek, and we stepped outside the cathedral into a foggy, farm-smelling street. I could hear time giggling like a schoolgirl somewhere close by, and the mist amplified and distorted her every echo. Gas lamps shone ethereal through the haze, from which passers-by emerged like startled spirits. We ducked into a tavern on the porticoed *Plaça Major*, where I explained the problems I was experiencing with time to Josep. The priest chuckled and stirred his cortado. 'Time is no man's friend, Señor Gaudí … and she'll wait for no man either.'

'So how am I meant to track down time?'

Padre Josep smiled. 'My dear Antoni … only God has a handle on time, God and nature, for they alone are infinite.'

Worried by these words, I fasted myself into a wholly intentional delirium. In my feverish dreams that night, the dark-haired Josefa Moreu was telling me she loved me, but I was distracted because I saw time peeping from behind the wizened wishbone branches of the two trees in front of our family home in Riudoms. 'I love you like the sun, the moon, the stars,' Josefa said. 'I love you like the ocean,' she said. But I didn't reply because I was too busy watching time, determined not to let her out of my sight on this occasion.

My young niece, Rosa, tempted me out of my starvation with rustling bags of roasted *castanyes* and soft marzipan *panallets*. In our turreted Barcelona house, I'd show Rosa my latest architectural drawings and tell her about my hunt for time, while Papa frowned silently from his armchair by the fireplace. By day, I busied myself by designing some odd-legged chairs for Señor Güell, and I drew the altar for the monastery at Montserrat. Then, with a stroke of either luck or genius, I decided to make a trap for time by securing the commission to design *a really big church.*

'It's going to be a temple, Señorita Moreu,' I told Josefa when we met for afternoon tea at the Hotel Eixample. Josefa fidgeted with her prim lace collar and checked her slim gold watch. Unlike my dream version of Josefa, the real Josefa wouldn't look into my eyes, and I was left staring at pieces of her, like the tiny mole under her left ear and the cup of shadow at the base of her neck. I showed her del Villar's blueprints for *La Sagrada Família*, which I had drawn over with firm black ink, and Josefa's lashes lowered in concern. 'But ... what's this, Señor Gaudí?' she asked, indicating the curving spectacle of the central nave.

'It's inspired by nature, Señorita Moreu, so it won't be dark and full of torment like those other churches. Joyous nature in her abundance has informed every element of the design. Look here ... see the wonderful curve of the pillars ... like branches.'

'But church pillars are *straight*, Señor,' Josefa said, touching the pearls at her neck.

'Yes ... but there are no straight lines in nature, Señorita Moreu,' I told her, hearing the twang of desperation in my voice and feeling the tug of Josefa's affection receding from me, like the tide rushing away from a shore. Just at that moment, time went gaily gliding past the window on a yellow unicycle and blew a kiss at me. I looked away.

Shortly after that, Josefa stopped replying to my letters. I started to pray the rosary three times per day, to attend Mass in the Gothic cathedral every noon and to fast on Mondays and Fridays. I designed *Casa Milà* with its wave-like façade, seaweed balconies, lily-pad flooring and spiralling cockle-shell staircases. I built *Casa Batlló* with its undulating sand-dune roof, which I brightened with smashed-up ceramic tiles into a feast of colour. One sweltering June day as I worked on the meandering sea-serpent in *Park Güell*, I felt time running her cool fingers along my earlobes, and I kept my dear friend Padre Josep's words in my head, 'Remember, Antoni, only God and nature are infinite ...'.

After some time, I received a letter from the city council:

DEAR SEÑOR GAUDÍ,
ONCE AGAIN YOU HAVE EXCEEDED CITY LIMITS AND WE, THE COUNCILLORS, ARE OBLIGED TO TELL YOU TO STOP. THE CITY OF BARCELONA WILL NO LONGER PERMIT YOUR WILD FLIGHTS OF FANCY TO SCAR OUR CITYSCAPE. IT MUST STOP. IN FACT, WE REMIND YOU THAT WE ONLY EVER ASKED YOU TO DESIGN THE STREET LAMPS IN *PLAÇA REIAL*, AND LOOK WHAT HAPPENED ON THAT OCCASSION. DID WE ASK FOR FLOWERS? NO. DID WE ASK FOR LIZARDS? NO. DID WE ASK FOR A SOLDIER'S HELMET WITH A SNAKE COILING AROUND IT AND DISSECTED EAGLES' WINGS GROWING OUT OF IT? NO! WE NOW ASK YOU, SEÑOR, TO DO THIS CITY A FAVOUR AND JUST *STICK TO THE BLOODY PLANS!*

I ignored this correspondence of course, tacking it to the wall of my studio. Decades passed, and my church began to take shape. Human lives were short compared to the life of my creation. Long after Josefa's hesitant glances were but a memory, and both Rosa and Papa were gone from this life, I moved into my workshop in the crypt of *La Sagrada Família*, where I lived and breathed amongst the dust of my creation. I prayed the rosary nine times per day. I fasted each weekday from dawn until dusk. I even threw away my smart coats and tried dressing in rags and growing a long matted beard so that time would mistake me for a beggar and pester somebody else. But it was all to no avail. Time continued to mock me relentlessly.

Occasionally, some bewildered local residents would come down the steps, stick their top hats around the doorway of the crypt and cough, 'Ahem … Señor Gaudí? … Do you have, eh … a completion date … roughly … in mind?'

My answer to them was always the same. 'My client, Señors, is God…. And as far as I am aware, He is not in any hurry.'

Really it was only the apprentices who knew, or had guessed, how long this project would take. I saw the weight of lifetimes carried in each man's eyes. I sensed a heaviness about their limbs, and I realised then that Time had chained herself around their necks and was taking gleeful piggybacks on each man's shoulders. Shocked by the blatant rudeness of Time's behaviour, I would slam things down and throw things about and shout a lot to try and scare her away. I soon got a name for being short-tempered, which was unfair really.

At some point in the early twentieth century, I died. You'd think that dying would be something a person would remember, that it would stand out from other memories of breathless autumnal strolls in *Parc del Besòs* with Josefa, or the day I threw a plaster-of-Paris jug at that young apprentice,

Jaime, because he had ruined all the ultramarine tiling on the balustrade. But I have to admit that I have no recollection of dying at all. I can only suppose that it must have happened shortly after I got hit by that tram car on *Corts Catalanes*. However, I didn't waste too much time worrying about this because I soon discovered that when a person is trying to catch something that is impossible to catch (like Time), there are distinct advantages to being dead.

I was now able to pounce on Time as she lay asleep on the steps of *Mirador de Colón*, or swipe at her while she was teasing the salty-fingered fishmongers in *La Boqueria* market. But I could never quite catch her, and in an infallible counter-move, Time had a tantrum and blew herself up in the middle of Spain, halting building work on *La Sagrada Família* indefinitely. Then, in an admittedly brilliant follow-up, Time detonated herself in the centre of Europe, starting a world war that put construction of my basilica on hold for more than a decade. Not content with these initial sabotage attempts, Time then destroyed my original models and plans, staged six acts of deliberate arson and two lootings, hired three inept architects and placed my church on the main route of a high-speed underground railway.

And yet my stone-winged phoenix continues to struggle from the ashes, like the human castles of Tarragona summers, where the *pinya* weave their arms tightly together as the tiny *enxaneta* climbs to the top, and the crowd gasps, wondering if she's going to fall. These days tourists line up around the block for a chance to step inside my incomplete church. I sometimes spot Time standing in the entrance queues, licking a 99 ice-cream, wearing a Barça FC cap, or posing for photographs with American families. Occasionally she waves or sticks her tongue out at me, but as soon as I step closer she disappears behind the plump limestone arse of a singing cherub.

'Why don't you give it up, Tío Antoni?' Rosa asked me as we sat together in the fronds of an unkempt palm. But I just shook my head.

It is incompleteness that fascinates us. Poles never reached. Liners lost mid-ocean. Hands almost held. Skins almost touched. Nearly completed spires paused on their ascent into the Barcelona sky. And a church under construction for more than a century. 'When will it be complete?' the tourists are always asking. But only Time will tell, and she for the moment is jumping up and down on the yellow cranes surrounding the basilica, trying to get them to break. Meanwhile I wait, drifting in and out of shadows, sitting on the mosaic salamander in *Park Güell*, or resting my aching bones on the glittering dragon-scale terrace of *Casa Batlló*.

Crushed

Ezekiel was born eleven months after Kingsley. This was the first mistake. Had there been more than a year between them, they wouldn't have both ended up in the same class as Shanika Burke. And perhaps none of it would have happened.

The Obinwanye brothers had both been born in Dublin. But when it was International Co-operation Day 2002 at Edenmore Educate Together National School, someone handed Ezekiel a Nigerian flag and told him to hold it and smile. All his classmates were holding different flags, and the only kid who had an Irish flag was Shanika, even though everyone knew she'd been born in London. 'Right, guys, big smiles,' their teacher, Mr Weldon, had said. But Ezekiel didn't want to smile when he was holding that shitty Nigerian flag. So, on their International Co-operation Day display, all the other kids were smiling, and Ezekiel was pursing his lips as if he'd just swallowed a spoonful of Aunt Hadiza's sour tomato stew. It bothered him whenever he walked past that picture. He would have smiled if he'd known Shanika was going to see it.

In the next mistake, in 1995 Jonah and Blessing Obinwanye had moved from their Gardiner Street flat to the new suburb of

Edenmore, when Kingsley was three and Ezekiel was two-and-a-quarter. Making yet another error, the Obinwanyes rented a flat on Hunter's Run, one of many abandoned Edenmore roads leading to nowhere. Black tread-marks arced across the deserted streets. Nights were full of revved-up engines. Apartment complexes resembling high-security prisons blocked out the horizon. A hard easterly wind blew perpetually across the barren floodplain on which the suburb of Edenmore had been raised, as far from the city as it was possible to go without tripping into another county. Out here, you could be in Dublin, or at the edge of any city on Earth.

The next mistake came halfway through this morning's local history lesson. Mr Weldon had been explaining how the entire area of Edenmore had once been owned by some Arab prince, who'd bred lithe black Byerley Turks, gleaming chestnut Darley Arabians and white-flashed Godolphins on this land. The prince's second wife was Rita Hayworth, after whom many of the Edenmore roads-to-nowhere had been named. Hayworth Run. Rita Vale. Hayworth Mews. Photos that Mr Weldon google-image-searched on the interactive whiteboard showed a drowsy-looking redhead, chin propped on one knuckle, long-lashed gaze lowered, as if mulling over a Sudoku puzzle. Ezekiel wondered what your woman would have thought of having half an unfinished Irish suburb named after her. He didn't reckon she'd have been too impressed. This thought made him snigger again, to which Mr Weldon shouted, 'Right, that's it, Ezekiel. Last warning. Outside. Now. And put your name on the red traffic light.'

Ezekiel stomped to the back of the class. He moved his name sticker from orange to red, slammed the classroom door and skulked out into the corridor. This was the next mistake.

INNIU

And then Ezekiel sees the knife. He's been charging headfirst into the January dusk, fingers fretting a clump of fluff in the pocket of his hoody. Shanika's scream pierces the static groan of the M50, and reaches Ezekiel just as he's about to turn into Hunter's Run. He swivels on the heels of his Adidas runners and looks back across the scrubland.

From here, Shanika and Kingsley look like actors on a distant screen, caught in a pool of orange streetlight. Scruffier. Smaller. Shanika's damp red hair is making an estuary down the back of her pink bomber jacket. Her purple hi-tops are tied in rough white bows. Her jaw grinds nervously. Her cheeks are crimson-pinched. She's staring towards the yellow grit box, beside which Kingsley and the white stranger are flinging their hands at each other. Faces confrontationally close. White runners circling. At thirteen, Kingsley is a head smaller than his classmates. Than most people. So he spends his life glaring upwards in confused defiance.

From the acute angle of Kingsley's jawline, and the violent shapes he's throwing in his Ireland hoody, the forthcoming fight has just become inevitable. Again, a glint of dying sunlight catches something sharp between Kingsley and the two white strangers. Something Kingsley hasn't seen. Ezekiel starts to run.

AMÁRACH

Tomorrow, Ezekiel will stay home from school. His mum will sit on the red IKEA sofa, hugging her sides and moaning Igbo incomprehensible to him. The aunties will genuflect around her as if she's a newly venerated shrine. Rosary beads will run through their fingers like tears of glass. His sister, Faith, newly arrived from Galway and trying to look brave, will keep making cups of tea that nobody drinks. Yesterday was the Feast of the Epiphany. The aunties will read great significance into that.

After handing him a lunch of reheated jollof rice and burnt fish fingers, Ezekiel's mum will send him to the Spar shop for a half-litre of semi-skimmed milk. The two-euro coin gripped in his sweaty fist, Ezekiel will hurry through the labyrinth of Edenmore under a bone-coloured sky. Walking at a followed-at-night pace, he'll take the dirt track across the scrubland of Hunter's Green. Fortressed by red-brick starter homes and weathered duplexes. A full moon will hang amidst the clouds, like a punched hole in the dirty white page of the sky. What if he could see through the moon hole into the nothing beyond? Is that where Kingsley is now? Ezekiel will shrug away the thought. And he'll jog home, stumbling over the mossy grass, forgetting the milk.

When he slams the door of flat 53 and leans against it, eyes bulging, Faith will be saying to his mum, 'You sent Ezekiel out for milk? On his own? What is wrong with you, Mum? Jesus. Is one son not enough?' In the living room, the aunties will have lit even more candles. Even more incense. So it will seem as if the flat could combust at any minute into a lavender-scented inferno.

Ezekiel will shuffle into his bedroom, kick off his runners and think about how each family has its own smell. An encoded combination of washing powder and skin cells. Each family member has their own scent, a further encoding of sprays and sweat. But you can't smell your own skin. The box room that the Obinwanye brothers shared for eleven years will now smell exclusively of Kingsley. As if Ezekiel is an odourless ghost.

Shivering, Ezekiel will crouch on the lower bunk bed, his back to the greying primrose wallpaper. Whenever he closes his eyes, he'll see Kingsley's face, as if the image is projected on the pink grape-skin lining of his eyelids.

Open eyes: the empty bedroom.

Closed eyes: Kingsley's face.

Two days after his nineteenth birthday, Ezekiel will leave home and rent a flat by the Royal Canal. He'll get a job as a cashier in a Maxol station whilst working towards his business studies degree. His troubled sleep will be soothed by the rhythm of the night train, but he will never get used to sleeping alone. At twenty-two, he'll meet a South African woman called Hope. His memories of Kingsley will surface most strongly whenever he gives his firstborn son, Emmanuel, the night feed, and the newborn's tiny determined fist closes around his father's thumb.

INNÉ

For the first eight years of her life, Shanika was an only child who conducted whispered conversations with herself, and seemed to inhabit a parallel world. Stooping in the sweet-smelling autumn of St James's Park, she would collect conkers and group them into families, giving each a name. At three, she had a pet spider called George who lived in a webbed corner of her bedroom. At four, she refused to go to bed without first being carried out into their Croydon backyard to say goodnight to the moon. These mild bouts of precociousness were endearingly tempered by her frizzy red hair, weak chin and eyes of apologetic blue. At seven, her parents moved home to Dublin and bought a house in Edenmore. This was the beginning of the problems.

When she was eight, in a coup Shanika never quite got over, her mum gave birth to Aoibheann, a ferociously photogenic sister, who came into this world hollering and protesting. Bewildered, Shanika watched her parents' attention shift, like the arbitrary sweep of a lighthouse beam, drawn by the demands of this colicky baby, who threw up each night onto the lino of the master bedroom. Aoibheann's presence stained into the floorboards of their starter home on Hayworth Mews, seeping into the foundations.

Years passed, and not until this morning did thirteen-year-old Shanika experience again the sensation of being completely wanted.

'Finished already?' Mr Weldon had said when she'd handed up her local history project. 'I've a special job for you so.' And he'd taken her to the corridor, where she was to help Graziana, their Sicilian SNA, to put stickers on all the new pencil pots.

It had been nice, sitting in the corridor, listening to Graziana's musical chat. But already the SNA had been summoned to the Senior Infant classroom, where one five-year-old had stabbed another with a compass. So, Shanika was sitting alone in the echoing corridor, fingers becoming tacky with sticker gunk, when Ezekiel catapulted from the classroom. They stared at each other. Cats in a dark alley.

Ezekiel was tall. Long-limbed. Always slightly pissed-off-looking. One Big Break, she'd watched him nick a skipping rope off one of the infants. He'd started skipping, the rope flicking around his head like the almost-invisible blur of bluebottle wings. Then he'd handed the rope back to the gobsmacked infant and slouched away as if nothing had happened. Many times Shanika had seen Ezekiel step coolly between his brother, Kingsley, and some adversary who was clearly about to flatten him. Kingsley, laid back, short, good-looking, never seemed particularly grateful. There'd been some weird thing with Kingsley a couple of years ago. She'd felt bad when he got in trouble. She just hadn't been prepared for him to lunge at her like that.

'Shit,' Ezekiel looked away from Shanika and kicked the skirting board, 'I'm getting outta here, you wanna mitch?'

To her own surprise, Shanika said, 'Yeah.'

INNIU

Shanika sees the knife before anyone else. She sidesteps behind Kingsley, eyes scanning the deserted street. 'Who's the big man now?' one of the white guys leers as he flicks the knife between his thumb and forefinger.

The sun has set, and the icy Edenmore wind singes Shanika's earlobes. Street lamps have just come on, glowing hot cherry-red before turning to orange. A Dublin bus labours past, carrying rectangles of steamed-up light through the darkening street. The white guy slides the knife back into the inside pocket of his leather jacket. For a second, Shanika thinks everything will be okay.

AMÁRACH

Next week, Shanika will ask her mum if she can stay off school for another day, but her mum will reply, 'Not today, hun. I've to take Aoibheann to her piano class, and you can't stay here on your own. Things have to get back to normal, love.' She will kiss Shanika's forehead just above her left eyebrow. 'Come on, you didn't know that Obinwanye boy that well, did you?'

Dropped off at quarter to nine, Shanika will tightrope-walk across the windswept tundra of the yard. A few infants will be playing clapping games that will be carried by the hard Edenmore wind. *A sailor went to sea, sea, sea, to see what he could see, see, see.* On the roof, the Irish flag and the muted blue Eco-School banner will lap and twist. At the infant end of things, parents will push their buggies to and fro, talking in low voices with their arms folded. They will stop talking when they see Shanika, and will kneel to zip their kids' skittle-bright coats to their chins. *But all that he could see, see, see.*

A woman in a pencil skirt will step from the congealed map of parents and say, 'Shanika Burke? Can I ask you a few questions, pet?' Someone (Shanika doesn't know who) will intervene, and she will be steered by the shoulders towards the flat-roofed magnolia L-shape of the main school building. She will be led past the glass-fronted reception, Blu-Tacked with Head Lice Warnings, Healthy Eating posters, and the latest Anti-Bullying Policy, translated into seventeen languages, and into the sickbay, from where schoolyard shouts will echo as if she is trapped in an empty fish tank. Left alone, Shanika will lift a bottle of Calpol from the nurse's station, click open the childproof lid and down a mouthful of the pink syrup.

Three years later, Shanika will be sitting in a brown leather armchair with her hands folded in her lap. 'And was it soon after that the anxiety started?' a therapist will ask. Sixteen-year-old Shanika will nod and stare out of the therapist's window. By this point she will have returned to her private world of named conkers and pet spiders. 'And soon after that, your mum and dad separated, is that right?' the therapist will ask.

'Yeah,' Shanika will answer, 'and I moved with mum to Tallaght.'

'And how did you find the move?'

'Grand,' Shanika will reply, staring out of the window and swivelling the armchair. A grey-headed gull will pace the top of a nearby street lamp. Somewhere below, someone will be playing a guitar. The therapist will charge Shanika's mother seventy-two euros for the two-hour session.

Soon after this, Shanika will develop a taste for Iron Maiden and will dye her hair black. She will start to write. She will finish her first novel at the age of seventeen and keep it in a shoebox under her bed, where her mum will pretend not to know that it exists. She will title it *Pieces of Fire*. She will never show it to anyone.

Her early twenties will be spent falling in love with indifferent men, who will not love her back. When she is twenty-four, a different therapist will ask, 'So, Shanika, would you say that these issues started around the time of this incident on Hunter's Run?'

'Maybe,' Shanika will answer.

The therapist will make a note on his pad before asking, 'And did you ever talk to Ezekiel again?'

INNÉ

Kingsley was held back in Junior Infants. This put him in the same year group as his brother, Ezekiel, despite the eleven-month age gap. Kingsley reacted to this situation by refusing to answer his name when the register was called. Tearing the staples out of all his copybooks with his teeth. Overturning metal-legged tables whenever he was asked to do anything. Emptying pots of crayons and crushing them into the grey-flecked heavy-duty carpet. Getting into fights whenever possible. Routinely smashing the fire alarm in the cloakroom, instigating his own series of impromptu fire drills.

At six, he was prescribed methylphenidate and allocated a resource teacher. When he was seven, Shanika Brady joined the class. She sat beside him and arranged her four rainbow-striped rubbers in lookout posts around her desk space. And because her quiet presence made his heart do a breakdance inside his ribs, and because she smelt like morning milk and coconut shampoo, and because the flecks of warmth in her eyes were the colour of Mars bar caramel, Kingsley lifted one of Shanika's rubbers and soundlessly snapped it in half, leaving crumbs of rainbow-coloured plastic on the Formica table. This, he reckoned, had established some kind of bond.

That school might have thought Kingsley was stupid, but he was smart enough to cop when his gangly brother, Ezekiel, started getting all dopey-eyed around Shanika. He might not have been able to write shit, or reel off his times tables backwards like Ezekiel, but he could read what his brother wanted, just like he could tell what mood his mum was in when they got home before she even spoke. So this morning, when Ezekiel was sent out of the classroom, Kingsley remembered that Shanika was also in the corridor, stickering the pencil-pots. Without causing a fuss, Kingsley stood up and followed his brother. It was too easy. This was the great thing about being seen as stupid; teachers had zero expectations of you.

Kingsley stepped into the corridor just in time to hear Ezekiel saying 'You wanna mitch?' and Shanika saying 'Yeah.'

'Cool,' Kingsley said. 'Where we going?'

Ten minutes later, with expert tactics developed over many years of mitching, Kingsley aimed for the fence on the windowless side of the building. Ezekiel and Shanika tagged behind him. They cut across the vegetable plot, where trellises divided barren strips of earth into twelve class plots, ravaged by the same wind that raked the yard relentlessly. Fools these teachers were, Kingsley thought. There was more chance of growing pineapples on O'Connell Street than of anything taking root in the vegetable plot of Edenmore ETNS. Each summer, the infants' marigolds failed to raise their ruffled orange lips farther than a few millimetres above the cracked earth. And on the sixth-class patch, cane crucifixes waited for sunflowers.

'Come on, lads,' he beckoned them under the wire fence. The feeble January sun smeared traces of pink above the pigeon-grey rooftops of Hayworth Estate. Playing a game of Would You Rather, they jogged out of the open school gate, across bright pelts of verge, giving way to rubble where even nettles struggled to sprout their fuzzy stems. *Would You Rather eat a spider or kiss Marcella from fifth class? Would You Rather jump out of a plane or swim with alligators?*

Skirting the rusty signpost for the not-yet-built railway station, they continued past the boarded-up, sand-blasted façade of Shangri-la Manor, where the Arab prince would have lived with yer woman Rita Hayworth. At the back of the house was an abandoned orchard. Tree trunks twisted like grey fusilli. Uneaten apples dropped onto the gum-pocked pavement, where they rotted into pursed brown sacks. All the ivy had been ripped from the manor, leaving shadowy patterns up the walls and making the house look somehow naked.

Two white guys were leaning against a red van parked outside the manor. One of them made monkey noises, and his friend laughed. Kingsley gave them the fingers, 'Losers.'

'Fuck off back to Africa,' the taller guy snorted.

'We're not from Africa. We're from the ...'.

Ezekiel tugged his arm. 'Leave it.'

Slowing to a speed-walk, they continued down the flimsy abandoned film set of Edenmore Main Street. Past the Spar and the Paddy Power. Past the boarded-up entrance of O'Leary's pub. Past Rzeszowska Bakery, its swing-doors wafting hot, doughy *makowiec* goodness into the cold street. Past the quasi-historical granite plinth with no names carved on it, a memorial to a war that hadn't yet happened. At this safe distance from the school, they stopped, leaning against a house-end. Shanika grabbed her hair and looped it into a ponytail. She popped a strawberry chewing gum into her mouth. 'So, what we gonna do next?'

INNIU

Earlier, from across the street, leaning on their battered red van, they hadn't looked that threatening. Now, up-close, Kingsley can see the soulless glint in their eyes. Grey tracksuits and shaven heads. Greyish skin, like something dead already. 'You owe us a fuckin' apology.'

'What a douche,' Kingsley mutters, rolling his eyes. Shanika shuffles closer. Chlorine in her hair. Strawberry on her breath. Streetlights turning red to orange.

The taller of the two white guys prods Kingsley's chest. 'You owe us an apology, mate.'

AMÁRACH

After Small Break tomorrow, the pupils of Edenmore will gather in the sports hall to conduct a minute's silence. This, the principal has decided, is the appropriate mark of respect.

The principal will stand at the front of the hall of children, head bowed, concentrating on breathing. And she will think: will the Parents' Coffee Morning have to be rescheduled? How should she handle things if that clot of sixth-class girls currently wavering on the edge of collective hysteria at the back of the hall were to lose control completely? Would removing them from the hall be insensitive? But on the other hand, were she to allow them to stay in the hall, would their collective hysteria cause a tidal wave of emotion, which would filter down to the bewildered infants cross-legged at her feet? How would she respond to a hall of three-hundred crying pupils? Are any of the children counting? Do many of them remember how long a minute actually is? And would any of them notice were she to shave ten seconds off?

INNÉ

In the next mistake, Ezekiel stood on the edge of the diving board, from where the slick heads of the swimmers bobbed around like seals. Outside the glass-walled swimming pool, the light was already fading. It had taken them over an hour to walk from Edenmore to the National Aquatic Centre, making a detour to the Burke flat on Hayworth Mews, where Shanika had shoved a bright spaghetti-tangle of togs into her backpack. ('These are me brother's, he won't mind if you borrow them.') They'd walked the roaring dual carriageway of the Edenmore tributary road, which circled roundabouts and led eventually to Blanchardstown Shopping Centre. From there, the National Aquatic Centre was a ten-minute uphill climb. Kingsley had mock-staggered the last five minutes, clutching his heart as if mortally wounded, to which Shanika scoffed, 'Ya eejit, Kingsley.' Then they'd sat at white tables in the Aquatic Centre Café, slurping cokes and munching two-euro punnets of salty swimming-pool chips.

And now, Ezekiel's toes playfully held and released the edge of the diving board, while his eyes followed the wet gleam of Shanika's navy swimming cap as she pushed off from the deep end in her red swimsuit. Shanika was a pretty crap swimmer. She struggled falteringly across the pool in an uncoordinated breaststroke that seemed to involve being dragged backwards as well as forwards with each pull. Her thin white arms grasped at the water, while the wavering outline of her froggish leg movements kicked feebly against the blue. A lump rose in Ezekiel's throat. The water could swallow Shanika so easily. She could simply disappear into the turquoise pool. Yet she pressed on, as if magnetised by something.

It was only as Shanika neared the shallow end that Ezekiel saw what she was swimming towards. Like a rock star in his Jacuzzi, Kingsley leaned against the pool wall with his arms spread along the navy-flecked tiles. Shanika swam up to him, and with one fluid movement, which might have been another stoke of her ad-hoc swim, she slid up his body and kissed him on the cheek. They both laughed. Ezekiel couldn't hear the laugh, but he could see it. In his head, the pool went silent. Blood pounded in his ears, making him temporarily deaf. A sudden flush, like biting into a chilli by accident. This could not be real. It was as if he were outside his body, looking down on this skinny Nigerian-Irish kid on the end of a diving board, watching Shanika swimming back towards the deep end, shallow ripples spreading into V-shapes in her wake. A heat came into Ezekiel's throat. He clenched his fists and jumped.

Forty minutes later, icy air rushed up at him when he stepped out of the Aquatic Centre. 'Come on, Ezekiel,' Kingsley shouted. Behind rainclouds, the sun had set. The Edenmore wind now carried a knife-edge chill. The schools were out; strings of kids trailed across half-finished streets, halting the school traffic. Ezekiel trudged behind the others, hands in his soggy pockets. His scuffed runners followed branching tarmac fissures, over greying splats of gum and ground-in, skeletal leaves.

Kingsley and Shanika walked in front, singing some stupid pop song in shouty, out-of-tune voices. As they crossed the tributary road, Shanika skipped up beside Ezekiel. 'Carry me bag for a sec?'

'No,' Ezekiel replied a little too loudly, 'fuck off.'

Shanika stopped, a crease of hurt etched between her eyebrows. 'Suit yourself.' She turned away, a slather of her damp hair whipping his cheek. Kingsley strolled back towards Ezekiel, painfully cool, hands in the front pocket of his Ireland sweater, a gentle smile on his face.

'Hey, man.' Kingsley slapped Ezekiel's shoulder. 'What's up?'

Ezekiel's hands were shaking. 'Don't. You. Fuckin'. Talk. To. Me. Okay?'

'Whoa!' Kingsley laughed, 'just chill, man.'

'I don't wanna chill.' To Ezekiel's mortification, he could hear tears in his voice. 'You think I didn't *see* you and Shanika? You think I didn't *see*?'

Kingsley ducked his head and rubbed the back of his neck. 'Ah, man, come on … you know that was just for the craic like.'

'I'm taking the shortcut.' Ezekiel turned and stumbled tear-blinded across the stony earth.

'It's dodgy that way!' Kingsley shouted. 'Don't go that way. Come on!'

But Ezekiel kept on walking, and soon the roar of the nearby M50 overpass swallowed Kingsley's shouts. Ragged-winged crows circled the estate, and a moth-eaten tabby slunk out of an alley with a sparrow in its mouth. When he reached the middle of the field, Ezekiel looked back and saw those two white guys from the morning coming down Hunter's Run in the direction of Kingsley and Shanika. Bad luck, he thought, to bump into those weirdos twice in one day. When he looked back again, he saw Kingsley with his hands spread wide, and one of the white guys jabbing the air in front of his chest. His instinct was to sprint across the green to watch Kingsley's back as usual. But then he thought of Shanika in her red swimsuit, and he turned and kept on walking homewards, through the thorny undergrowth towards Hunter's Run. This was the last mistake.

INNIU

Running through melting sand. Running through falling water. Running against the weight of an Edenmore gale that might have billowed across centuries, through the manes of chestnut Darley Arabians and white-flashed Godolphins. The Feast of the Epiphany. And on some level, Ezekiel knows he'll be running across this field his whole life. Running, and never getting any closer to where Kingsley is falling. And Shanika is shrieking, backing away from blood already oozing into pavement cracks. Still, Ezekiel keeps running. And knowing. And running.

AMÁRACH

In fifteen years, three months, two days and seventeen hours' time, Ezekiel will glance down at his mobile as he's walking up O'Connell Street and he'll be greeted by the royal-blue silhouette of a Facebook notification. *Shanika Burke has sent you a friend request.* Ezekiel will stop at a zebra crossing. He'll tug his tie loose and undo the top button of his shirt, which will feel suddenly tight.

Black balloons will pock the sky, handed out by a theatre group barricaded around the Spire. At the top of Henry Street, a dreadlocked man will be crouched on his hunkers, drumming a catchy rhythm on an assortment of pots and pans. Nearby, a scrawny man in a limp leather jacket will shout, 'The day is coming! Judgement day is close at hand!' Outside the GPO, a pro-life group will be setting up stall, struggling against the warm, petrol-tasting wind. One of their posters of a tiny, coral-fingered zygote will flit on the breeze and wrap around a limestone pillar near Ezekiel. He'll think that today feels like the end of the world, for some reason.

Reaching the top of O'Connell Street, Ezekiel will continue walking and will turn into the Garden of Remembrance. He'll lean on the blue-painted railings and watch two sisters running around the rectangular pool. The younger of the two, a toddler of maybe three, will be wearing a ballerina-style get-up of pink gauze and mesh. Running around the Memorial Gardens, her yellow wellies singing a clip-clap-dunk-thunk rhythm on the concrete. Her older sister will follow at a protective distance, already with that too-wise look some children have.

When he first met Hope, they went through that bartering phase of love, when past hurts are traded for future loyalties. He'd told her about Kingsley. Silent tears had coursed her face. He'd imagined they'd always be able to talk like this.

Ezekiel will look to the granite swans at the top of the gardens, their beaks stern against the bright spring sky, their wings arching. Twelve years of Kingsley's face projected inside his eyelids. And now Shanika. *You have a new friend request.*

On a balcony, on the other side of Dublin, Shanika will shiver under the wheeling screech of gulls. She'll take another sip of her decaf. Glancing at her phone, she'll think: I shouldn't have sent that. From here, the indigo curve of the Dublin Mountains will resemble the wheeled-in backdrop of an old western. Growing up in Edenmore, she'd never realised there were mountains so close by. In the hotel bedroom behind her, there will be a suitcase waiting to be packed. Clothes will be strewn like archipelagos across the soft beige carpet. A ticket will be waiting to be double-checked before a pre-dawn flight to Sydney. But for the next thirty-five seconds, Shanika will stand beside papery trumpets of fading daffodils, thinking about Ezekiel Obinwanye, wondering if he will answer.

Acknowledgements

Unending thanks to my parents, Valerie and Gerry, and to my sister, Alice, for their constant love and encouragement. Thanks to Dave Lordan, who told me I could write, and to fellow writers Llaura McGee, Charlene Putney and Sheila Armstrong, who insisted that I must. My sincere gratitude goes to the team at New Island Books; thanks to Dan Bolger for asking the right questions, and to Justin Corfield for meticulous attention to detail. I'm grateful for the help with translation I received from Keitaro Horii and Garry Bannister. Thanks to all the editors who took chances on my work in its early stages; to Hubert O'Hearn for being my first real fan, and to Sinéad Gleeson for being such a great champion of Irish women writers. Lastly, loving thanks to my husband, Richard, for helping me realise that real life is the best story I will ever write.

'Infinite Landscapes' first appeared in *The Long Gaze Back* (ed. Sinéad Gleeson). An earlier version of 'Titanium Heart' first appeared in *Fugue: Contemporary Stories* (The Siren Press, ed. Lucy Carroll). An early version of 'Under the Jasmine Tree' received an Honorary Mention in the

Bath Short Story Award, and was published in the *Bath Short Story Award Anthology 2014*. 'On Cosmology' was shortlisted for the Hennessy New Irish Writing Award 2016, and was published in *The Irish Times*. 'How to Learn Irish in Seventeen Steps' was first published in *Young Irelanders* (ed. Dave Lordan). 'Death and the Architect' first appeared in *Unthology 7* (ed. Ashley Stokes).